HEIRESS OF STARS

KINGDOM OF FAIRYTALES: PETER PAN BOOK 2

ANNE STRYKER
J A ARMITAGE

Edited By Rose Lipscomb

Cover by Enchanted Quill Press

Proof Reader: Tina Merritt

❀ Created with Vellum

KINGDOM OF FAIRYTALES

You all know the fairytales, the stories that always have the happy ending. But what happens after all those storybook characters get what they wanted? Is it really a happily ever after?

In this prequel, you will find out what happens next, be transported back to those lands you fell in love with and be prepared to meet some new characters along the way.

Kingdom of Fairytales is a new way of reading with one chapter a day and one book a week throughout the year beginning January 1st

Lighting-fast reads you won't be able to put down

Read in real time as each chapter follows a day in the life of a character throughout the entire year, with each bite-sized episode representing a week in the life of our hero.

Each character's story wrapped up at the end of every season with a brand new character and story featured in each season.

Fantasy has never been so epic!

READING ORDER

Kingdom of Fairytales is a 52 book series split into thirteen seasons. Each season has a four book story arc of a fairytale character with the last season seeing them all coming together. You can read any series first with the exception of thirteen, however it is recommended that you read in the order below...

PREQUEL

SLEEPING BEAUTY

1. Queen of Dragons
2. Heiress of Embers
3. Throne of Fury
4. Goddess of Flames

LITTLE MERMAID

5. Queen of Mermaids
6. Heiress of the Sea

7. Throne of Change
8. Goddess of Water

RED RIDING HOOD
9. King of Wolves
10. Heir of the Curse
11. Throne of Night
12. God of Shifters

RAPUNZEL
13. King of Devotion
14. Heir of Thorns
15. Throne of Enchantment
16. God of Loyalty

RUMPELSTILTSKIN
17. Queen of Unicorns
18. Heiress of Gold
19. Throne of Sacrifice
20. Goddess of Loss

BEAUTY AND THE BEAST
21. King of Beasts
22. Heir of Beauty
23. Throne of Betrayal
24. God of Illusion

ALADDIN
25. Queen of the Sun
26. Heiress of Shadows
27. Throne of the Phoenix

28. Goddess of Fire

CINDERELLA

29. Queen of Song
30. Heiress of Melody
31. Throne of Symphony
32. Goddess of Harmony

ALICE IN WONDERLAND

33. Queen of Clockwork
34. Heiress of Delusion
35. Throne of Cards
36. Goddess of Hearts

WIZARD OF OZ

37. King of Traitors
38. Heir of Fugitives
39. Throne of Emeralds
40. God of Storms

SNOW WHITE

41. Queen of Reflections
42. Heiress of Mirrors
43. Throne of Wands
44. Goddess of Magic

PETER PAN

45. Queen of Skies
46. Heiress of Stars
47. Throne of Feathers
48. Goddess of Air

URBIS
49. Kingdom of Royalty
50. Kingdom of Power
51. Kingdom of Fairytales
52. Kingdom of Ever After

URBIS PRISON
SHIPLEY
THE VALE
AZREN
BADALAH
DESERT
KISBU
DRACONIS
ZHORE
MOSA
ABORIA
ELDER
AIRE
SKYLA
AZURE
ENCHANTIA
URBIS
EMERALD CITY
OZ
FLORIS
TULIS
THE FORGE
ARCADIA
RENAIS
MELFALL
ATLANTICE
ANTLA
W
E
S
KINGDOM
OF
FAIRYTALES

11TH NOVEMBER

One moment, the night enveloped us in a pitch-black haze. The next, light bled into my eyes, burning my retinas and making me almost fall out of the sky. I blinked violently against the building tears, certain they came from discomfort and blindness, not from the sensation of my world being ripped away.

A hand caught my arm, stopping me in the air. "Look down," Bay said.

I pulled my attention away from the sky and squinted at a beach. Sunlight hit the golden sand like it was glass, spewing rainbows across shallow shoreline pools. High grass, filtering into dense, menacing woods, waved in a warm breeze. I could make out jagged outlines rising in the distance, but a wash of deep green covered everything as we descended.

My feet touched the ground, and I released a breath. "This is it?" I turned slowly, taking in the never-ending cerulean sea. It stretched into the horizon and then dropped off. I was half-certain it ended where the light no longer could be seen glinting off the water.

"It's beautiful, isn't it?"

I wrung my hands before dropping my arms to my sides and facing the treeline once more. "Freedom has never felt so bittersweet."

"Bittersweet," Bay repeated, "that's a good word for this place. Lovely and lethal. We really should get moving."

Spinning on his heel, he headed toward the darkest shadows in the ominous foliage. My gut tightened, but I followed him. "Do you have a safety guide? Any tips, tricks, or comments you'd like to share that will help me stay alive long enough to find and defeat the pirates?"

"I do hope you have a plan to defeat the pirates. That would be my first tip."

"I'll figure one out once I see what I'm dealing with unless you already know?"

He picked up the pace. "Who? Me? I don't know anything."

I glanced over my shoulder. It took a conscious effort not to freeze on the beach. Out of the water rose a giant, bulbous head, easily ten times my size. Water streamed off the grey flesh in torrents. When I met the creature's single crimson eye, its beak clacked, and a suctioned tentacle lifted out of the foaming waves.

"Okay," Bay said with an edge of panic in the lilt of the word. "Maybe I know one thing. Run!" Snatching my hand, he tore through the grass, yanking me behind him just in time for the Kraken's arm to plunge into the sand at our heels. A divot remained, filling with rainbow-strewn water.

My feet pounded against the sand as it thickened with dirt, and Bay didn't slow when we ducked into the forest. Hundreds of green shades, some lightened by streams of sunlight, and others blackened by shadows, fled past us in a blur. Skye zipped along overhead, disappearing in and out of the branches like he'd done this before, and it hardly bothered him.

"A terrible place to land, really. Truly dreadful. We're lucky to be alive." Bay bounded over a fallen log in a manner that boasted the pixie dust still coating his skin. I tripped over it, stumbled, and only narrowly missed careening into the ground headfirst thanks to his firm hold on my hand.

"Can we—" I gulped air. "—pause for a moment?"

"Not yet."

"Why not?"

Trees cracked behind me on my left, and my organs leaped out of my skin as I jumped, looking back. A tentacle slithered through splinters back to the source like a snake to its nest. My blood curdled, bile rising. Bay merely, and calmly, stated, "Because we're still within reach."

My muscles were tense by the time Bay slowed and glanced behind us. Trees completely obscured the ocean from view, but he appeared to see what he needed to. Exhaling, he released me. "Welcome to Neverland."

Fearlessness painted his face in excitement that didn't fit the situation. A giant squid nearly crushed us five seconds after landing. What lay ahead if this was how it started?

I looked back through the trees, wishing the sickness in my gut would settle. What was I thinking coming here? That I could take on all the pirates by myself? Was I that naïve?

No, I knew better than that. I ran away. And I wouldn't pretend otherwise. Maybe a part of me thought if I avenged Whisper, the gaping hole in my chest would close, and I'd be able to breathe again.

Blinking back, and forcing away emotions that threatened to consume me, I clenched my fists and faced my guide. "What now? How do I find the pirates?"

"Well, we should probably make our way to one of my hideouts. That's where everything I need will be. And the pirates..." He whipped sweat out of his eyes and pushed his bangs back. "They generally find me."

"Comforting," I mumbled.

He shrugged, slipping his hands into his pockets. "After we get some supplies, I can take you to their nest if you'd like to see what you're dealing with."

Hugging myself, I rubbed my arms and positioned my back away from the ocean. "I don't actually know why you're here. You said you'd tell me if I came with you, but then..." *Things didn't quite go as smoothly as they might have.*

If I didn't focus on the ache in my soul, I could almost trick myself into believing Whisper was at home, waiting for me to make Skyla safe again. She'd run to me when I returned, wrap me in a hug, and hint that more happened between Bay and me than I would be willing to admit.

Damn it. I scrubbed a hand over my face, cursing the burning behind my eyes, throughout my whole head.

"Are you all right?"

"Yes," I snapped. "Just tell me why you're here already."

Bay stared at me in a way that almost made me feel guilty, but it was when he looked away that the sorrow deep in my chest called to the pain etched on his face. "I'm looking for something."

Deliberately, I softened my tone. "What are you looking for?"

"It's hard to explain, and we need to keep moving." He spun on his heel again, pausing before taking a step. Tightening his braid, he met my gaze. "Stay with me and don't wander off. Those are my tips and tricks to maybe surviving Neverland."

"Aren't you being a tad bit presumptuous? I doubt you could save me from that thing back there if we faced it head-on." I didn't have the strength to argue or press the issue, so I kept his pace.

"I'm nothing if not ostentatious, and unless I'm mistaken, I did just save you from *that thing back there,* so unless you fancy a swim, we'll never have to face it head-on."

"*Ostentatious*. Big, showy word for someone who hides in a treehouse, hating company. Are you sure you know what it means?"

He cast me a disapproving grimace. "You clearly do."

"Because I'm perspicacious when it comes to details and words."

"Indubitably."

A tiny smile touched my lips while we crunched through the forest, no path in sight. Skye zipped out of the treetops and settled on Bay's head. The tiny creature glanced at me, hummed something and zipped off again. He returned moments later, chirped something else and then lay down in Bay's hair.

Bay didn't reply, but his eyes peered into the distance, narrowing. "Watch your—"

He didn't finish the line before the ground fell out from under me. Pain exploded in my side, then frigid water submerged my head. I gasped when my mouth bobbed above the surface. The current yanked me back under. Squinting through the murky blackness, I saw nothing. Breaching the surface again, I sucked in another breath, using it to scream, "Bay!" Torrents ripped me downstream, slamming my body against rocks along the way.

Heat bloomed in my skull as I frantically did everything I could to reach air. The river had appeared out of nowhere as if the terrain had moved in the time it took me to take a step. Could that happen? Did that happen here?

Bay's stories had included numerous situations I never thought possible, so there was no telling what I would come to face. With Krakens living in the ocean, what could possibly dwell in inky black rivers that appeared out of forest floors?

I shivered with icy fear, fighting to see through the darkness. If I could just reach the bank… I had to. Rivers, if I wasn't mistaken, led to the ocean, and that thing was probably still waiting for its next meal.

Heart pounding, I fought the current. Stubborn, it thrust me beneath the water again, tumbling me around like a stray stone. I couldn't let it win. Not now. Not before I avenged Whisper and saved Skyla, then —then…

Then I didn't know what, but Whisper would never let me give in or give up. Holding an image of her smile and an echo of her laugh in my mind, I forced my battered and aching body to obey, to drag me one inch at a time to a cleft of dirt overhanging the rushing depths. I dug my nails into it, but the mud gave way. My legs scraped the wall, so I crammed my moccasins into crevices. Burying my hands again, I found sturdy roots and pried myself from the chilling rapids.

Collapsing, I stared up at the blackening tree canopy. Dread spun in my stomach, and I shot upright, feeling for my knife. It was still at my thigh. It was okay. Next, I found my sopping bag. The bread I had on me fell through my fingers in sodden clumps. My books were destroyed. My gloves, spyglass, and pan flute were waterlogged. But, hopefully, they would dry out, and... My heart sank as I lifted the pouch of pixie dust.

It flopped to the side, empty, all its contents lost to the river, annihilated in the water.

My hands shook from cold as I put everything back, and I jumped when the ground beside me slammed closed, the river gone like it had never been. A thin seam that almost looked like a scar in the earth was the only hint I had ever been at the water's mercy.

"Bay?" I called into the woods, tightening my jaw to avoid chattering my teeth. Only bugs and rustling leaves responded. Then, thunder.

The island quaked. A long-fingered bolt of lightning reached down from the sky, grasped Neverland, and rattled it. After the second impact, a downpour of rain burst from the clouds, hitting me like needles.

The force alone made it difficult to stand, but I

found my legs and staggered ahead. The trees broke shortly after to display a sky at war and a lone skull carved into the edge of the beach.

Skull Rock.

I knew it as though I'd always known it. Its ominous form seemed branded on my brain. Gaping mouth. Dead, hollow eyes. It offered nothing but an unsettling sensation—and shelter from the stabbing rain and raging sky.

I peered behind me, then at the ocean.

The grey water surged and crashed, blending with the horizon. Could I get that close to it, or would the Kraken come back?

An ear-splitting noise sent me hurtling forward. I whirled on the trees. Eyes bulging, I stared at an ashy trunk, sliced through the middle. Char washed off the wood to pool in the mulch on the ground. Lingering electricity crawled up my spine. The strike couldn't have been more than thirty feet from me.

"May the airwoman protect me from threats of sky and sea." Choking on the prayer, I dashed through the pelting rain into the maws of the cavern rock. Hand on my knife, I awaited glowing eyes, screeching laughter, silent footsteps, shadows, danger, death But only an empty pit with an ascending tunnel at the back stared at me. It couldn't really be safe. Could it?

I remembered a note on Bay's map of Neverland: *Watch out for Skull Rock after dark.*

It was dark—the rain hammered on, a rush of noise that clouded my mind—but it wasn't technically *after* dark. Unless time worked differently here, it had been dawn no less than an hour ago, so maybe it was safe until after dark? Would the rain last that long?

Would I?

My hand left my knife and clamped against my mouth. Shivers wracked my soaked body, every inhale burning down my throat. I was freezing. I was tired. Random patches of my skin stung in the open air; others ached from bruises. Neverland had swallowed me and spit me out minutes after I'd stepped foot on its soil. I wanted to scream, but my throat was too raw, my spirit too exhausted.

"Whisper," I managed through trembling lips, "help me." Those weren't the words I was thinking. She couldn't help me. Not now. The words I was thinking were *it should have been me.*

But it wasn't. So here I stood, alone.

And I had to pull myself together.

Slapping my cheeks, I gasped in a breath and ran over my options. I had to wait out the storm and find Bay, all before dark. Bay appeared to know this world, so even if the storm lasted past dark, I needed to be out of this cave before then in accordance with his notes.

Defeat the pirates.

Save Skyla.

Return…home.

My heart dipped, weighed down by the certainty "home" would never feel that way again. By now, Peter may have forgotten me. Tiger Lily and Whisper were gone. Maybe the Lost Boys would remember me if I made it back quickly, but their memory was little better than Peter's after a certain amount of time.

Overwhelmed, confused, scared, and above all else, cold to the bone, I leaned against the cave wall.

It vibrated. Leaping off, I turned around, and my eyes widened. The grinding sound of stone against stone filled the space as the skull snapped its mouth closed, leaving me in near-perfect darkness. The barest outline of light between the rock's jagged teeth did little to illuminate the space—until fire crackled behind me.

Scared to see what next awaited, I wrapped my fingers around the hilt of my knife, pulled it free, then slowly rotated toward the sizzling pops. Several torches lined the tunnel at the far end of the skull.

I swallowed, my throat dry. My heart thundered, its beats resounding through the tips of my toes. "There's no way I'm going back there," I whispered into the eerie, white noise of rain and thunder.

Stepping back, my moccasins splashed into a puddle. A trickle of light beneath the storm drew my gaze back to the skull's maws, and my stomach tightened. Water spilled in, filling the room at an alarming rate.

Did some cruel god orchestrate this horrific situation? Thrown about from one near demise to the next, I was doing all I could just to keep breathing.

The water reached my ankles, so I closed my eyes briefly, cursed Neverland, and started for the lit tunnel. The path ascended, curling, and I noted several ridges in the walls shaped like arched doorways. I assumed like the skull's mouth, the stone blocking the passages moved, but I didn't know how to make it, so I followed the path until it opened into a chamber.

Piles of straw threaded with silk and down lay before me. Random objects—chests, gold, broken plates, chair legs, mirror glass—sat neglected all around. Lightning crashed across a sky visible through two large holes and a smaller one between them, and...those were the skull's eyes.

This was something's nest.

My only consolation was that the chamber appeared, for the time being,, empty. I started for one of the piles of miscellaneous pieces, hoping the ivory bone I glimpsed wasn't human, but a tittering voice stopped me in my tracks.

"It's dreadful," the voice sighed, sending me hurtling toward the piles of straw. I tucked myself into a corner behind them and held my breath. If I had any luck left in me, the rain would mask my pounding heart.

"So you've said, sister." Three women entered the room. White gowns spilled over their slender bodies, beautifully contrasting with their dark hair and dark skin. But it was their incandescent wings that froze me in place. The pure feathers gleamed, drawing my eyes away from the spindly teeth pouring out of their mouths.

Sirens.

The eldest of them folded her arms, peering outside with a grace that negated her grisliness. "It's so rare we have visitors," the woman murmured.

My heart stopped, but she pivoted to face her sisters instead of looking at me.

"So many at once after so few in so long." The middle siren curled her lips back against her teeth in an appalling grimace. "It can mean nothing good."

"We know this," the eldest returned. "Since long ago."

"Still, it's..." Sorrow touched the woman's features, and she shook her head, glancing at the youngest sister.

Her bright voice was airy and kind despite her horrific maws. "I do love when Bay is back, though. He's terribly fun."

"Occasionally, overmuch." The eldest smiled, her teeth hidden, but the expression still sharp.

"The children say he has come with a girl this time." The youngest held her fingers before her lips. Deadly excitement sparked in her eyes. "Imagine that. Our Bay with a girl."

Icy shoots of fear trickled down my spine, raising all the hair on my flesh. I fought every instinct that screamed at me to run because I had nowhere to go.

"Already?" Both the others' eyes widened.

The eldest's lips parted. "It can't be."

"Oh, it is, though. I'm certain of it. She has hair like a sunset, and her eyes...they're ringed in gold the children say."

The eldest clasped her hands. Distress marred her face, and she turned toward the storm again. Lightning flashed across her defined cheeks, outlining the barest trace of panic. "We must find them before the worst occurs." Her eyes closed, her teeth clacking. "Come, sisters, the children are hungry. After they're fed, we'll send them to search for our Bay and the girl; we must make sure we are there in time."

Without flourish, the woman ushered the others from the room.

I stayed where I was, staring after them until my legs burned, begging to be stretched. Three sirens were after us, after me, and I was hiding right behind their beds. I squeezed my eyes closed in case it was all a dream, but my wet clothes clung to my skin, making me shiver so completely I knew it couldn't be.

I had to get out of here, even if it meant braving the storm.

Lightning cracked across the sky, drawing my attention to the only clear exits. If I could scale the rock face —or rock forehead—I could make it down the back of the skull and into the woods.

Inching toward an eye socket, I peered outside. Wind whipped rain into my face hard enough to leave welts on my cheeks, but I squinted against the torrents at the ocean. No creatures rose from the depths, but a bed of sharp rocks peeked out of the boiling waves.

Stay here with the sirens or be dashed against the stone.

My head swirled, so I ran my fingers through my wet hair, gripping the strands. Thunder rumbled in the distance like the great airwoman was laughing. I sneered. "You're Skyla's *lucky charm*." I lifted myself onto the ledge, gripping the stone until my nails chipped. "What could possibly go wrong?"

Rain beat into my side as I found a foothold. My moccasin skidded, and I clenched the rock, scraping my palms. One at a time, I pried my shoes off and secured them in my bag before locking my toes on the water-washed stone.

Water soaked everything but my dry mouth as I felt for a handhold, then delivered myself onto the curved forehead. One slow movement after another, I dragged my body above the skull's eye.

Rain stabbed my back; water rushed against me like

a river. I narrowed my eyes through the blur. Shaking violently from the cold, I nearly missed grasping solid holds every three movements, but by grace or luck or some other unseen force, I managed to reach the top of the skull's head.

The back of the skull wasn't as sheer. Piles of mossy stones descended like steps into the forest, but I still took my time reaching the ground in the tempest. Out of breath, I faced inland, leaned against a mossy boulder, and put my sopping shoes back on as though protecting my feet mattered much now. Even as the rain carried everything away, I knew my hands and feet bled.

I started ahead at a pitiful limp, daring the world to throw something else at me. I had no idea where I was going, if I'd ever find Bay, the pirates, my way back home, and I hardly cared at this point.

Everything hurt. Neverland hadn't simply swallowed me up and spit me out. It had chewed me up then regurgitated my remains.

Walking for hours in the pouring rain, half-starved was about as glamorous as it sounded. Thankfully, the lightning had died down some time ago, and the downpour had eased, but I still had no way to navigate through the thick woods.

Ambling in circles was exhausting, but Bay had mentioned twice how we needed to keep moving, so I supposed that was the least I could do. Not to mention, I feared if I stopped, the cold would set in beyond repair.

My fingers were stiff, and only memories of

Whisper kept me continuing forward. *She wouldn't want you to give up. She wouldn't want you to stop.* If I believed in an afterlife, I would have stopped back at Skull Rock and thrown myself into the ocean, but death accomplished nothing.

She wouldn't want that for you anyway.

"Right," I chattered, "but how exactly am I supposed to continue without her?"

I trudged on, pausing when the rain slowed. Could it really be letting up? I held out a shaking hand, hopeful. I had begun to forget what being dry felt like. Looking up at the sky through the canopy, I watched the dark clouds disperse. A sliver of moon loomed above, offering less light than the rest of the stars. They seemed closer than in Skyla, each twinkling brightly in the pitch expanse.

Had I really walked the entire day away?

As I stood there, staring at the sky, I knew it wasn't as unlikely as it seemed. Everything hurt. I was no stranger to long walks in the woods, or climbing, or getting caught in the rain. But all of it at once, plus running for my life, had strained my muscles and my mind.

No end lay in sight. I didn't know where I was going, how I would get there, or even, really, where I had come from. Glancing behind me, I witnessed nothing but wet trees and brush. Facing forward again, I clenched my teeth. It all looked the same.

My stomach swirled with hunger and unease. Could Neverland have put me in a loop? Could I be walking toward nothing, coming from nothing, ending up nowhere?

"Why do you hate me?" I whispered my throat raw with thirst. Surrounded by water, I hadn't thought to drink any, but I was parched.

Pressing my palms against my eyes, I teetered and shook my head. I had to keep moving. My foot took a step forward, but the world slanted off-kilter. Humming filled my head, the soft noises so calm, so comforting. My lips parted in a yawn that I succumbed to.

I fought to keep my eyes open and took another step. The world doubled, turning vibrant colors. Something was very wrong. Violet melded with emerald, dipping into shades of crimson and tangerine.

My back straightened. The sensation of something crawling on my neck held me steady in place even as everything around me tumbled into insanity. I reached back, plucking a long splinter from my skin.

"What?" I mumbled.

My vision failed. The touch of long fingers skittered down both my arms just before I collapsed in a wet heap on the ground.

12TH NOVEMBER

Movement. That's what woke me. Exhausted to my core, nothing short of being jostled like a sack of potatoes would have done the trick, so that's exactly what I felt like when I came to in someone's arms. Darkness still bathed the forest, washing everything I could see in muted greens and charcoal shadows.

I blinked at a smooth face, hoping to clear my mind, but it lagged, confused and not at all happy to be present right now. The person holding me was running. That was a good deduction. Where was the person going with me? Who was the person?

I squinted through the fog in my head. The face was handsome. His—definitely a his—hair was dark. A short braid hopped up when the person jumped. My senses crashed down on me.

"Bay!"

Bay startled, his hazel eyes going wide. He met my

gaze and stared, but he didn't stop moving. "You're awake?"

"Yeah, thanks to you. Think you could handle me a little more violently?" Relief filled my chest, and for the first time in hours, I could breathe again. "Because I don't."

He stayed silent. His eyes shifted from the path before us, to me, and back to the path.

My brows furrowed. "Put me down. I think I can walk." I hoped I could. My muscles were little more than goo at this point, and my bones were mush, but being carried like a princess didn't suit either of us.

"You're covered in bruises," he stated.

"White water rafting without a raft will do that to you."

When he didn't so much as hint at slowing to set me down, I shifted in his hold to peer over his shoulder. "Are we being chased? Where are you going so quickly?"

"Our base."

Our? The relief at seeing him trickled away, one droplet at a time, but my mind cleared more with every shock rattling through his bones to mine. I pursed my lips and narrowed my eyes.

He provided me half a smile, but something about it wasn't right. "What is it, Lyric?"

"Where's Skye?" Bay's clothes were dry, and it wasn't raining anymore. Here, especially here in Neverland with danger around every bend, he would be coated in shimmering dust, but not a single fleck touched his skin.

"Skye's waiting for us at our base."

No way would they be separated at such a distance. "Put me down," I demanded.

"But—"

"Now." I let my fingers drift to the sheath at my thigh. A cold wash of fear ran over me when I found it empty.

The wide-eyed concern painting Bay's face vanished. His hazel eyes flickered between the earth tones and a mustard yellow. He licked his lips. "If you insist."

My heart clenched. Bay hurled me into a tree. The impact cracked against my joints, sending piercing shots of hurt stabbing out through my nerves.

The creature's voice distorted, a mix of Bay's tenor and something entirely repugnant. "Better?" Sapphire caught my eye, and he flipped my blade into the air, catching it precariously. "Little Lyric,"—his form shifted. Sallow skin stretched over thin, protruding bones. Cracked teeth grinned at me, a blood-red tongue tracing each point—"so alone in the world."

I planted my hands beneath me, shoving the damp ground, but my muscles wouldn't cooperate. My arms shook like a baby goat's legs; then my face fell splat into the mud. "What are you?" I choked, turning my body so at least I wouldn't inhale dirt and mold.

"I'm your friend Bay." The creature's form transitioned, Bay's voice lilting in its words. "Or perhaps..." The words softened, turning feminine, and a mass of curly blond hair spilled over small, dark shoulders.

"No—"

She touched the tip of my knife, a coy smile lightening her face. "Perhaps I'm Whis—"

Her mouth went slack, and she tumbled forward, buckling in a heap of sallow skin and gangly limbs. I gasped, panting, starved for air. A long knife protruded from the creature's back. The thing's back. Not Whisper's. Not… But it felt like I'd witnessed her dying right in front of me. Again. So close, and yet again, I could do nothing to save her.

I scrambled in the mud, finding, at last, a way to pull myself off the ground. Pressing my back against the trunk behind me for support, I stared as a gleaming form dropped out of the trees and yanked the long knife out of the creature's back.

"Are you all right?" Bay asked. He wiped black blood off his blade and secured it before looking at me. I didn't reply. He took a step toward me. My heart thundered in my chest. "You're not exactly easy to track; I hope you haven't gone on any adventures without me." He stopped, and his attention dropped to the sapphire-encrusted hilt of my knife. It lay within the bony fingers of the creature still. Bay plucked it free and cleaned it off on his pant leg, floating over the corpse as if it didn't faze him.

I crushed myself against the trunk. "How do I know you're not…one of those things?"

"I suppose in the same way you knew that thing wasn't me." He flipped my blade, offering it to me exactly how he had when we first met. "It was a young one, that's for sure. Some of them can copy mannerisms, habits, and emulate a person based on recent memories far better than he could." Bay's head tipped down, his gaze darkening. "Also, I'm sure most other changelings know by now not to toy with my form."

I clamped a shaking hand around my knife's handle, met the briefest hint of resistance, then snatched it from him.

Skye flitted out of the trees to sit on Bay's shoulder shortly after I managed to settle my breathing. Concern marred the pixie's tiny brows and, admittedly, seeing him set me somewhat at ease.

"I suppose he was your first hint that something wasn't right." Bay smiled at his companion. "That's one thing you can always count on. If we aren't together, something is terribly wrong."

"Actually,"—I swallowed—"the first hint was you called me Lyric."

His brow quirked. "I haven't called you Lyric before?"

"Never once." Whatever strength kept me upright drained away until I was relying entirely on the trunk behind me to keep from collapsing. I couldn't dwell on this; I had to tell him about the sirens. My lips parted, but I never reached the words.

Bay had one arm at my back and the other at my knees before I knew where to start. He lifted me off the ground, not quite touching it himself. His lips thinned in a teasing smirk. "Goodness. You're lighter than you look. Are you made of air?"

My cheeks flushed. "I can walk."

"Clearly, you can barely stand." He floated up through the branches until the forest was a patch of green below us. "Besides, why walk when you can fly?" He shifted my weight so I could easily lay my head against his chest and murmured, "Rest for a bit, Wind

Song. We'll be in a safe place soon, and I'll treat your injuries."

I watched Bay's face, searching for anything that might be another Neverland trick, but he didn't so much as inch forward without my first accepting what he had said. He held my gaze, the depths of his eyes flecked with gold in the starlight, a gentle smile curving full lips. Only when I leaned my head against him and gave in to the darkness did I feel the soft breeze of movement against my skin.

I clung to his heat and that warm breeze, desperate for the image of Whisper crumbling in the woods to burn away. It didn't.

My eyes fluttered open, the space around me completely unfamiliar. Firelight cast shadows on the walls, and I realized they were dirt. Roots stuck out of the ceiling, the spindly fingers interlocking like spider webs.

Skye hummed, and I found Bay hunkered beside the fire, pouring over several maps. He looked up at me, his eyes alight in the glow. Coated in reflective dust, he appeared spectral, and I wondered for a moment when he floated off the ground if I were dreaming.

He touched my cheek, his hand, pleasantly cool. "How are you feeling?"

I assessed the bandages wrapped around my arms and legs. They had been skillfully bound, and I wondered how familiar he was with tending to his own wounds. Shifting in the bed of clover, I winced. "Everything's sore."

"After the trip you took, I'm surprised nothing's broken." He brushed the hair off my cheek, and it felt phenomenally good. I nearly sighed into his touch, but I groaned instead.

"I think sirens are after us," I croaked.

"What?" His hand drew away.

"Sirens," I repeated their sharp faces and angelic forms burned in my mind. "It started to pour after I escaped the river. When lightning crashed too close for comfort, I took shelter in Skull Rock. The mouth closed. It filled with water. I followed a path toward the back to the chamber with the eyes, and..." I felt sick.

"You went inside Skull Rock?" Shock masked Bay's face.

"I didn't have much of a choice, I—"

"You saw a skull-shaped edifice and thought, 'Hmm, that looks like a lovely place. Let me just pop on inside to wait out the storm?'"

"Lightning nearly hit me! It was the best option I could think of after being thrown downstream and nearly drowning half a dozen times. What else would you have expected me to do?"

He deadpanned. "Trace the river seam back so we could have met in the middle."

I bit my tongue on any snarky remark I was brewing. That, the most logical of thoughts, hadn't crossed my mind even briefly.

Bay laughed, shaking his head. "I'm not mad. You're a little worse for wear, but you're all right. We're a little set back, but we haven't been put out beyond repair. You were probably concussed just a bit." His brows crashed down, and he folded his arms, floating near so his face was just before mine. "Actually, you probably *are* concussed just a bit. How old are you? What's your mother's name?"

I frowned at him. "I don't have a mother." And I didn't want to think about what had happened to the closest thing I did have to a mother. Averting my gaze, I focused on the physical aches blooming all over my body to avoid concentrating on the emotional ones bleeding in my chest.

"Everyone has a mother." He sat back down, his legs crossed.

"Well, I never knew mine."

"Oh." The single word stilled the air in the space. Only the crackling fire continued its murmurs. Several heartbeats passed, then Bay cleared his throat, rubbed the back of his neck. "You're probably hungry."

My stomach growled at the mere thought of food. "I wasn't until you said that."

He chuckled. "It's a good thing I caught a real delicacy while you were asleep then." He dashed toward the fire, and I watched him warily, expecting a rat or a snake.

He returned with neither. I breathed a sigh of relief and forced my aching body to sit up and take the wooden bowl he offered. A leg of meat and a salad of what looked like weeds sat side by side. "What is all this?"

"Rabbit and greens. It's the best we can do out here most of the time."

"It's more than enough." I lifted the meat to my lips and savoured the gamey, perhaps slightly burnt, taste. The juice seasoned the salad, and though both could have used salt and herbs, it seemed a meal fit for royalty.

Before I had to ask, Bay put a cup of water in my hand.

"You're awfully accommodating for the Bay I know. Have you been switched out with one of those things?"

"A changeling? No." He hovered cross-legged above the ground. "Can't fly, them. Not an ounce of belief in any of their yellow bodies."

"Then, about the sirens…" I stared into my cup.

Bay waved a hand, dismissing it. "Don't worry about them."

"But they knew you, me. They know we're both here somehow, and they said something about sending 'the children' out to find us."

"They're nothing new." A wry smile tipped his lips as he glanced at the ceiling. "I know how to handle them by now. Time moves differently for us here. That is to say, it stops. Get it? *Never*land. Never grow up. I've survived this place for years, and you don't survive long if you don't know how to handle a handful of sirens."

"Is that why you don't know how old you are?"

"Never grow up. Never grow old. Neverland's curse is Neverland's blessing." He exhaled, setting the matter aside. "I charted a path to Pirate Bay. It's a three-day journey, taking into account feasible setbacks. It's been a while since I dared go near there, so I don't know what to expect."

"I do," I noted, finishing my food.

His brows rose. "You do?"

"Pirates."

He rolled his eyes, flopping down beside me on the clover bed. "Ha ha ha."

"You mean, 'har har har.'" I smirked.

"Congratulations." He adjusted his dagger belt, removing some of the larger sheaths and setting them aside. "You've offended every pirate on this island. Let's hope none were within earshot." He took my bowl and set it next to his knives, waiting until I finished my water to do the same with the cup. Afterward, he smiled. "Good eve, Wind Song."

My heart thumped. Seeing him so close, deliberately sleeping next to me, set my mind adrift in a realm of inappropriate thoughts. *Shut up. You're concussed.* My reprimand did little to train the stream of thoughts as I lay back down. I stared at the ceiling, lips pressed together, and tamed my breathing.

Moments passed. Minutes.

"Oh," Bay murmured, "do you have any idea which group of pirates you're looking for? I'd suggest not taking on all of them if you can help it."

"There's more than one?" I replied.

He rolled over to face me and propped his head in his hand. "Of course."

I moistened my lips, trying not to look at his. "You recognized the pirate on Skyla. Don't you know?"

"Maybe."

"Well?"

He traced my face and pulled the tie out of his hair. His braid spilled free over his shoulders before he settled back down beside me, crossing his arms beneath his head. "Hook's Crew."

I froze. "But Hook's dead."

"No?"

"He is. Peter threw him off his ship and flew it to Skyla before I was born." I faced Bay. Our noses were mere inches apart.

He scratched his cheek. "What did I tell you about pirates who appear to have died? Captain James Hook is more cunning than the whole lot of them."

"But how would he have gotten to Neverland? You can't expect me to believe he knows how to fly."

"There's always more than one way to get home." Bay's voice was quiet, his expression solemn. Then he cupped my cheek and smiled through a hidden anguish I couldn't place the origin of. "It's late, Wind Song. Putting all this information on a concussed brain is probably bad for you. We'll talk more in the morning, I'm sure."

Then, without another word, he rolled over and went to sleep.

I crawled through the hollow log out of Bay's underground base. My muscles complained with each movement, and I knew it was going to be a long day. When I reached sunlight, Bay helped me up, and I stretched my aching limbs.

The forest gleamed with colors.

Purples and reds and oranges bloomed beside blues and pinks and whites, not a single space lacking vibrant hues. "What is this?" I asked, watching an iridescent butterfly as it perused the florals.

"Neverland after a storm." Bay hovered about a foot off the ground, his ankles crossed. He braided his hair and tightened the tie. "This was kind of an impromptu stop. My main base still has the supplies we'll need to move forward, so we have to backtrack a bit. I already accounted for the delay."

"I'll need the time to heal some anyway." I smoothed my finger down a delicate petal. A single dewdrop built and plummeted to the earth. "How worried should I be about another river swallowing me today?"

"I don't think we're passing any more river faults." He fished a map from his bag and scanned it quickly. "Nope. It should be a calm day."

I gripped my satchel's strap, thankful it and all of its salvageable contents had dried out by the fire. "Is that my definition of 'calm' or yours?"

He rolled up his map and stuffed it back in his own bag. "Why would they be different?"

"Well, mine is a 'none of the kids fell off the island today' kind of calm. Yours is a 'I know how to handle sirens if I cross paths with them' kind of calm."

He scoffed. "They'll never find us that quickly."

"How reassuring."

He held out a hand for me. "I think so."

I stared at his fingers when they wiggled.

"Are you coming?" he asked.

Skye sat on his shoulder, staring at me. There was a very distinct challenge on his little face, and I wasn't sure if he was daring me to accept or threatening me to decline. Taking a breath, I slipped my hand into Bay's. The pixie didn't move. Softer than I could catch, he murmured something in Bay's ear.

"Right," Bay grumbled, landing. "At this time, we'd be

too visible from the sky. If possible, I'd like for the pirates not to know we're here yet."

Skye nodded, flitting into the air. He swirled around my head several times, then returned to Bay's shoulder.

Bay smiled, his hand not having released mine. "It is good to always be able to fly here, though."

Lifting off the forest floor, I reveled in the sensation of nothing holding me down, and nothing pressing against my bruised legs. It was good to be able to fly anywhere.

We started through the colorful woods, Skye zipping in and out of the treetops as was his habit. Whenever he stopped in with us, he'd douse me in more dust, sit on Bay's head, or flutter along at our sides, then he was off again.

"Where does he go?" I asked sometime during mid-afternoon. The sun streamed through the trees, outlining a trail of dust as it sifted through the air to greet the ground.

"He's visiting the others," Bay replied.

"The others?"

"Other pixies." He held a hand above his eyes and stared up through the canopy. "I suppose you can't see them, because it's not like in Skyla. Pixies here remain well-hidden since there are so many dangers."

"There are pixies here too?"

Bay grinned. "Why would that surprise you?"

"I don't know."

"Truth be told, they were here first." He passed a tree, skimming his fingers over the bark. "There was a time when all of Skyla's islands rested in the sea. But the time before the pixies is an age near forgotten."

I could hardly believe that was true. Thinking about Skyla not floating made my stomach clench. It wasn't right. "Why did they leave here?"

"Why do most people leave their homes?"

I left to protect mine, but once I was done, I'd be returning. Since the pixies had remained in Skyla, they couldn't have left Neverland to protect it. It dawned on me. "Because it isn't safe anymore."

Bay pursed his lips and nodded. "Yep."

"How do you know all of this?" My brows knitted. "You return to Skyla like you live there and have bases here like you're just trying to survive some quest. Yet, you know all of these secrets and seem to be a walking encyclopedia of Neverland's history."

"Are we prying again, Miss Nosy One?"

"Don't be an ass, Star Boy." I wanted to know more about him. Everything else in my life had fallen apart. So—as scary at it seemed to consider—this boy I'd only known a little over a week was the closest friend I had left. And I knew nearly nothing about him.

Perhaps some of the desperation I felt showed on my face because he dropped his smirk and ruffled his hair, tossing flyaway strands out of his eyes. "All right. I suppose it's not a huge secret." He huffed, stepping over a fallen tree and continuing to float over the bushes past the decrepit log. "I was born here."

My eyes bulged; my heartbeat stilted. "What?"

He laughed, but it sounded unnatural. "Sorry. Not born. If I was born here, I'd age here. I was born in Skyla, but I was conceived here and raised between both Skyla and Neverland. Only one group of people like us ever lived out their lives here, and they're gone now. Everyone else you meet—the humans I mean—they're wanderers from other lands. We're all just cheating death, for a little while, or as long as we dare."

All my thoughts blanked with those words. He had been raised in both lands? How had I never met him before? Normal people rarely ever traveled to the outer islands that didn't have bridge walkways. His had been a new island for me, but surely Peter had known about it. Peter, at one point or another, knew everything...it was just a matter that he forgot. Had he allowed Bay to cross between the worlds? Did Peter know about Neverland? If he had once, did he remember it?

Bay poked me in the forehead, ripping me from my spiraling thoughts. "Don't look so shocked. Of course, a magical place like this has some pretty deep history."

"Sure. But you're tied into it." And, somehow, so was Skyla.

Bay flicked his gaze across my face, then turned away. "Someone has to be." His whole demeanor changed in the next moment, those foreboding words forgotten. Pulling away a weeping branch, he displayed a cove with a crystal blue pond. "Here we are."

Water spilled over a sheer rock face directly ahead. The rainbow mist touched my face even at this distance. Lush green grass coated the clearing, tiny flowers springing up all around. Rose vines laced before the tree line, as though they were holding the forest back.

"It's beautiful," I breathed, stepping foot into the space only after Bay landed there and let the willow branches fall back over the entrance like a curtain.

"You can wash off in the falls. I should have an extra set of clothes you can wear." He grabbed my arm, examining his bandage work, then nodded. "I'll redress these too."

"Is this place safe?" It looked as much, but the beach and the forest had seemed that way mere moments before both had tried to kill me.

Bay scanned the cove, secrets and memories spilling into his eyes. "Safe?" he whispered. "It's home." Looking down, he smoothed his fingers across his leather dagger belt and started for the waterfall. "I'll get you that change of clothes."

He slipped through a crevice behind the falls, and I followed, pausing when I saw what lay beyond. A cave space opened up before me, a log cabin sitting on aquamarine stone. Light scintillated through the falls to wash over the house in colored ribbons.

"This is incredible."

Bay smiled at the front door. "Is it?"

We both entered a quaint living space with a sitting area on the left and a food preparation area on the right. Stone counters, wooden utensils, and light cabinets more luxurious than anything I'd ever seen adorned the kitchenette.

Bay crossed between and entered a hallway with two doors, opening the nearest one. I only glimpsed the bedroom briefly, but it felt more like Bay's treehouse than the rest of the cabin. Papers, trinkets, and bookshelves displaying random odds and ends decorated the interior.

He emerged after a few moments with a linen shirt and a pair of trousers, not at all unlike what he was currently wearing. "I think I have some soap in the kitchen."

"Do you live here alone?" My eyes drifted to the untouched door, and I already knew the answer by the drastic differences between the single room treehouse and this place. It had a woman's touch. More than that, it had a family's essence.

So, where was his family?

"Not always," he replied, setting the bundle of clothes in my arms. The expression on his face begged me not to press further, but how could I leave it at that?

"What happened?" I floated over the counter dividing the kitchen from the rest of the room when he started searching through the cabinets under an empty water basin.

"That's none of your business." The words stung even though he'd said them so pleasantly.

I swallowed the bitterness resting on my tongue and held my head high. "I hate to inform you, but this is what a desperately wanting to know someone looks like."

He rose with a bar of soap, approaching. I hovered a foot above him, so he looked up as he took my hand and placed the soap there, wrapping my fingers around the waxy bar. "You're desperate to know me?" he asked, his tone seductive.

"A little." My face heated, and I tried not to think about his lingering touch.

"Why?"

My chest pinched, a lump catching in my throat. If I expected him to answer me honestly, I had to offer him the same courtesy. "Because—" The words were neither easy to think nor say. "—you're the closest thing I have left to call a friend."

The moments passing afterward took ages. He stared at me, every second building in my heart and making it beat faster. It was childish, wasn't it? Of course, it was. I was stupid, desperate, and alone—exactly like the changeling had said.

Before I had the chance to pull away in my own embarrassment, Bay floated up so he was taller than me and wrapped me in a hug. I didn't know what to do, so I clutched the clothing bundle and the soap until I was certain the bar had an imprint of my fingers.

"You're the first human to call me that in years," he murmured, his breath fanning past my ear. The same lonely, desperate tone echoed in his voice.

Dropping the clothes, I threw my arms around him and squeezed, biting back the emotions threatening to choke me. I didn't know how long we stayed like that in one another's arms or who pulled away first; all I knew was that when we met gazes again afterward, his eyes were glassy, and his cheeks were stained with tears.

13TH NOVEMBER

"Is this a good idea?" a soft, masculine voice pried open my dream and plucked it apart. I didn't recognize the person's voice, though something about the rise and fall was familiar.

"We don't have much choice. I'm open to other ideas, but if not, we have to try." That was Bay.

I stared straight ahead at the wall from where I lay on the couch in the cabin's sitting room. Bay and someone else were just behind me. Some wooden bowls shifted against one another, and I knew they were in the kitchen.

A long pause stretched before the other person responded, "We don't know if it'll even do any good. Lyric is...well. It's not like Neverland has offered her much kindness so far."

That statement was so true I felt it in my still-healing limbs, but why were Bay and a stranger talking about me?

"What do the other pixies think?"

The person scoffed.

"Well?"

"Yeah, okay, fine. There's *something*, but that doesn't mean it's anything we need. She can't even understand us, despite living with Tink all this time. Children lose their ability to understand; adults don't gain it. It's like flying." The person sighed deeply. "*Faith* and trust, Bay."

"Well, she has enough faith to fly," Bay grumbled, sincerely sounding wounded. "And you've been away from your kind since you were an infant. Maybe there are things you don't know."

"I'm not going to argue with you."

Bay laughed sardonically. "Skye, that is *exactly* what we're doing."

My heart thudded. *Skye?* Their conversation made a world more sense, but at the same time, it didn't. If I was hearing *Skye's* voice, everything they were talking about was invalid. I had to be dreaming. And yet, I was too scared to move and check.

The hushed tones and topic made it clear I hadn't been invited to eavesdrop, and I didn't know what would happen if they realized I was awake.

"I told you I was against this back when you first thought it up. She's only here because she lost her friend, and I think she has a chance against the pirates. But I don't want to see her, or anyone else, get hurt over a speculation." Anger built in Skye's tone. "Enough people have gotten hurt for our family."

"Ah, I see. You like her." Footsteps started away, drifting toward Bay's bedroom.

Before their voices disappeared behind the door, Skye mumbled, "As if you're one to talk."

When the door opened and closed, I released a breath, gasped in another, and clenched my jaw. *What?* The word screamed in my brain again, *WHAT?* No. No, I was dreaming. I shot upright, ready to pinch myself, but pain ricocheted throughout my limbs at the abrupt movement before I had a chance.

Okay. Not dreaming. At least not anymore. I may have been hallucinating?

A murmur of conversation I couldn't make out continued in Bay's room, and I knew hallucination wasn't right either. So, what was right?

Bay needed me for something dangerous, and Skye was against using me because it might not even work. *What?* I scrubbed my hands over my face, but there were too many holes to fill in, and my mind was still groggy with sleep. Pieces of their conversation, likely important bits, had already faded into the confusion.

I needed air.

My gaze shifted to the front door, and I peered between it and Bay's room. The voices had died down now, leaving nothing but the consistent white noise of the falls. My heart hammered when I stood and tightened the rope belt that held Bay's pants around my waist.

This past day had been nearly as bad an emotional ride as the river was a physical one. What would I do at this point if I couldn't trust Bay? Crossing to the door, I kept that question in my mind, along with the image of his tear-streaked face. If he needed help with something, even something dangerous, didn't he know he could just ask? That's what friends did, helped each other. Even after death, my motivational force was Whisper.

A twinge of soul-crushing pain choked me as I pushed my way out into the cave and slipped past the waterfall. Misty spray washed over my cheeks, cooling them in the gentle night breeze. Right now, I didn't care if being out here was safe; at least I could breathe.

Starlight glimmered off the pond, the moon invisible to my eye. It felt as though I could see for ages, and I wondered if one of those twinkling stars was really Skyla in disguise.

I moved away from the noise of the falls and into the murmur of the evening. Cricket song highlighted the buzz of other insects and hints I couldn't place. A creature zipped across the pond, snatching water as it passed. I squinted, tense, but settled when I realized it was just a pixie.

My eyes widened, everything stilling. The hints beneath the crickets and insects were voices. Soft, lilting voices. All at once, they chimed like bells—as they always had—but now, when I concentrated, I could make out words. Language.

I jerked back when a pixie darted before my eyes. She wore a little leafy skirt and a flower petal for a shirt. Her laughter was distinct. She flitted away, returning with someone else and pointed at me. "I scared her. Try it. It's fun."

Her companion made a twisted face, sticking out his tongue, and I blinked, honestly and truly terrified but for completely different reasons. The male pixie laughed too. "She isn't very fiery. I wonder if she'd run away if I touched her hair. Do you think it burns?"

My lips parted, closed, and parted again. I'm not sure how I managed to stay still when the male pixie shrugged and said, "I'm going to see," before diving into my locks.

Other pixies gathered around me, and I spun when something tugged on my shirt from behind. An elegant pixie with violet hair smirked. "She's wearing Bay's clothes. I do wonder what that means." The sly woman caught several of the others' eyes, and I flushed when they erupted in giggles.

"Bay has never brought anyone here before."

"She smells like something special. Magic?"

"She must be special to him."

Was I? Or was I a means to an end?

They continued, ignorant of my thoughts. "Do you think they're in love?"

"I wonder."

I went deathly still because that reply wasn't a pixie. Pivoting slowly, I found Bay with Skye seated and looking bored on his shoulder. The little pixie met my gaze and averted his eyes.

"What are you doing out here, Wind Song?" Bay asked.

The pixies buzzed, dashing toward him and running through his unbraided hair, tugging on his clothes. A few crawled between his dagger belt and his tunic, laughing when he loosened the strap and gave it to them.

"I, uh…" My gaze followed the handful of pixies who were spinning around with his belt. One tiny creature had managed to pluck a knife out, cover it in dust, and wave it about like a massive sword. "I needed fresh air."

"You look like you've seen a ghost."

Heard one, rather. I nearly blurted everything, but I stopped just in time. If I couldn't trust him, I shouldn't let him know I could understand the pixies. I may need to know what he and Skye are saying without them knowing. Swallowing my words, I settled on a lie I could easily pull off. "I had a nightmare."

"A nightmare?" His smile faded. "About...?"

All I had to do was drop my gaze to the damp, flowering grass at my feet.

"Right," he murmured.

"Is she okay?" a pixie's voice zipped past my ear.

Another gasped. "Bay, she's going to cry."

"Hold her." That turned into a chant. "Hold her! Hold her!"

Bay let loose an exasperated breath, stopping in the middle to address me. "Sorry, that was for them, not you."

"What are they saying?" I asked, peeking at him from under my lashes.

Their voices tripped into giggles.

"That he loves you!"

"He should hug you!"

"Kiss!" That one also turned into a chant, and I hoped Bay didn't connect it to my reddening face.

"Nothing," he grumbled, "important."

"Rude," Skye chimed, smirking.

It took everything within me in that moment to continue feigning ignorance, because this—hearing them, being a part of the secrets and the jokes—was thrilling. Is this what it was always like for Peter? Is this why he always had half a smirk on his face whenever he left the treetops? This was incredible and magical, more real and special than being dubbed “Skyla’s lucky charm” could ever manage.

It was inclusive instead of isolating.

Or it would be if I could make sense of what Bay seemed to be planning. For the moment, I was in on their secret, but my own kept me from saying so.

“It’s going to be a long day tomorrow.” Bay yanked me from my thoughts. “Why don’t we head inside and try to get some more sleep?”

I nodded dumbly. Bay skipped off the ground, clasping his dagger belt from the pixies, who complained. Snatching his floating knife out of the air, he returned to the grass before me and smiled.

I wanted to believe in that smile, but then I caught the troubled look on Skye’s face and knew I couldn’t. Silently, I followed him back inside, bid him goodnight, and suffered through an uneasy rest.

14TH NOVEMBER

Light shimmered in through the window, falling across my eyes. Still exhausted from the night's events, I resisted waking up until I heard a shuffle of paper.

Bay sat in the window seat with his legs kicked up, studying a sheet of parchment. His hand flowed over the page, long strokes, precise. His brows lowered with concentration, and it seemed as though nothing could break him out of the moment. Was he creating a new map?

He glanced up at me, and the spell broke. "Wind Song. Good morn." His eyes dropped to the page before him, then flicked back up. "I hadn't realized you were awake. Did you sleep well?"

No. "Well enough. What are you doing?"

"I was going over today's course." He cleared his throat, shifting the pages against the square of wood that served as a drawing table. "I may have gotten distracted."

Prying myself from the comfort of the couch cushions, I crossed the room and looked over Bay's shoulder. The now-familiar map of Neverland sat in his lap, but the usually vacant ocean in the top left corner held a sketch of a young woman.

Long lashes framed the woman's closed eyes, her mid-length hair spilling over her shoulders in a disarray that boasted rest. My heart dipped into my stomach, unleashing a swarm of butterflies in my gut. "Who's that?" I whispered.

Bay ran his fingers through his free hair, ruffling it as he tilted his head. "I thought I'd done a pretty good job. You really can't tell?"

My voice came out tiny, embarrassed. "Is it me?"

"Phew. That's good. A career as an artist is still attainable for me, then."

"But,"—I took a breath, looking over the delicate shape of the woman's cheeks, the peace, the full lips, the small nose—"she's beautiful."

Bay's brows crashed together, and he pinned me with a perplexed stare. "Yeah?" His lips pinched. "I mean..." He ruffled his hair again, pulling his attention back to the image on the page. "I'm not sure how to respond to that. Would you have preferred I'd drawn you ugly or something?"

When I thought of beauty, I always thought of Whisper. Her dark skin, petite fullness, and coy smiles. Self-consciously, I tugged on my pin-straight hair and knew instinctively it didn't contain the volume Bay had drawn it with.

"For the airwoman's sake." Skye's chirping voice made me blink out of the hypnotic state I'd fallen into.

The little pixie settled onto Bay's shoulder, whipping aside strands of Bay's hair, and sighed. "You're hopeless."

"It is a near-perfect likeness, isn't it?" Bay responded, puffing out his chest. Skye rolled his eyes. When Bay popped out of the window seat, he nearly threw Skye off his shoulder. "We should probably get some breakfast, pack our supplies, and head out if we want to expedite our demise at Pirate Bay."

"Wait." I swallowed when he paused and quirked a brow at me. "After we reach this 'Pirate Bay,' then what? What about what you're looking for? Will we find it on the way, or..."

Bay rested his drawing table against his side. For a moment, it looked as if the weight of an island rested on top of him, then it was gone. "I highly doubt we'll find what I'm looking for in the next few days, though I suppose anything is possible. Once I take you to the bay, I'll tell you some of the ropes, then, I suppose we'll part ways. Pirates don't really like anyone, but they really, *really* don't like me, so the quicker I'm in and out, the better." He took a breath, a grimness to his expression that made my heart bleed. "I'm sorry. I can take you there, but I can't help you past that."

"I understand." My chest twisted, uncomfortably tight. Did this mean he had decided against using me for whatever it was? Was I not good enough in the end? Somehow the thought of parting ways hurt more than the idea of not being useful. "Thank you for risking so much already."

He swiped his hair back and released a breath, turning toward his room. "What are friends for?"

. . .

A staleness coated the air, silence consuming the clearing as we stepped into it. After a day and of walking with scrapes and bruises, I had finally begun to heal enough that any aches from our traveling distance seemed minuscule.

Bay hadn't asked anything of me, and as far as I could tell, we were heading in the right direction. Perhaps I had dreamed the conversation from before? Or maybe they'd just decided against whatever they were planning. There was no way to know until we parted ways.

"Neverland weeps," Skye murmured, and I forced myself not to pause at the foreboding tone. I'd never heard a pixie sound so dire before. "We shouldn't have come this way. You can't still be—"

"No, but we've avoided it for too long." Bay turned his head away from me, quieting his words. "Whatever we're missing is here. I'm going to check, with or without help."

"I don't like this." Skye shot off into the trees, and Bay sighed, smiling when I sent him a worried look.

"What's going on?" I asked. "It's…" Tense? Still?

"Silent?" Bay swept his gaze over the clearing. Swiping a hand across his mouth, he released a shaky breath. "Yeah."

The space opened the further we went, and I glanced back at where we had come from. None of the full color that had decorated the forest lingered. Weeds patched the ground. Roughness thickened the dirt, making it appear coarse.

Skye zipped back and hovered in front of Bay's face. "No one's up there. Still. *We should not be here.*"

My heartbeat accelerated, but I forced the building fear down. "What's wrong?"

Bay looked between us, then shook his head. "Nothing. It's just a bad memory."

Skye's eyes narrowed. They stared at one another for several long moments, and I waited to see who would win. In the end, Bay passed the pixie and continued through the menacing air.

Skye frowned after him, looked at me, then sat on my shoulder and crossed his arms. I watched Bay's back, following slowly. "What is this place?" I whispered, more to Skye than anyone else.

The little pixie merely snapped, "Insufferable," and glared away.

I followed Bay, glad that at least Skye seemed on my side with whatever was happening but concerned that the tiny pixie would be little help if any danger appeared. The farther we went, the less I thought danger would appear. Like Skye had said, Neverland wept. More than that, it mourned. I could feel the ground almost tremble with sobs and had to focus on keeping my feet.

Nothing actually moved, but the sensation rocked my chest, connecting with the ever-present ache of losing Whisper.

That's when I saw them.

Protruding from the ground in great heaps were ivory bones. I froze where I stood, my eyes separating the mounds into individual pieces. There had to be hundreds, each and every femur, tibia, and skull picked clean like they had been resting here for years.

A tiny hand pulled on my hair, and I looked at Skye. His blue eyes stuck on the mountains of bone, sorrow etched deep in the crevices of his gaze. "You don't have to," he whispered with a softness that conveyed he didn't think I understood him.

Gathering my strength, I moved again, walking forward. Sickness laced the back of my tongue, and my stomach clenched. I anticipated a rotting scent to carry on the breeze at any moment, but only the same stale air wheezed in and out of my lungs.

This had happened so long ago now, not even death retained its hold.

"Bay," I called ahead.

The boy stopped where he was, and his chest shuddered with the breath. "Yes?"

"What...what happened here?" I reached his side and found dome-shaped homes slanted before us. Most of the structures had been knocked over or burned. Charred wood crumbled in a permanent state of decay.

"I told you before that a group of people like us used to live here. And that they were gone now." His face remained a solemn mask. "The pirates tricked them into a false sense of security, ambushed them, and slaughtered everyone."

A lump closed off my throat, but I managed a soft, "The pirates?"

"Hook and his crew. Few of the others saw reason to torment the natives like this. They were peaceful, dwelling among themselves, helpful when the situation presented the need." Bay looked at me, and chills ran over my body. Even though his face was young, his eyes bore a tale of an age past appearance, an age weighted with pain. "Culture and history that goes back to the beginning of Neverland died on this soil."

Closing my eyes, I felt that. Suffering and loss seeped through the thin leather of my moccasins, telling a story without words. "Why are we here?" My voice was raw, accusing, and I knew it, but I sided with Skye. *We should not be here.* This place was sacred, and if Neverland was willing to throw me into a river and nearly strike me with lightning for no reason, I didn't want to think about what would happen if I defiled this grave.

Bay nodded toward a stone structure. Large, painted blocks piled into a pyramid that shot into the sky, towering above the broken homes. A single dark entrance had been carved into the monolith. "I need to look in that."

"You *what?*" The monument was no less than a temple built beside hundreds, maybe thousands, of deceased people. "You're not serious." He said nothing. His expression didn't change. "I can't let you do that."

Bay's brow quirked, doubtful. "You can't *let* me?"

What was I saying? For all I knew, this was his culture, and he had every right to visit the temple of his ancestors. Insistent, I bit my lip. "No."

"Well, then. I can't let you stop me." He turned, facing the temple. "Skye, are you coming?"

"No."

"I'll be a few minutes, at the most. Skye says he'll stay with you since you seem a little shaken." Bay lifted off the ground and zipped through the entrance before I could hope to stop him. At best, I threw up my hand, opened my mouth, and stood there like a wounded statue, watching him disappear into the darkness.

Lowering my arm, I sighed, wincing at the bones when I faced them. "I'm not shaken," I murmured to Bay, though I knew he couldn't hear me. And, of course, that wasn't what Skye had said.

"We're both shaken," Skye mumbled.

"I can't believe he's doing this."—I chose my words carefully, pursing my lips—"unless, this is his ancestry."

Skye laughed shortly. "It's really not."

My brows furrowed, but I murmured, "I hope that was a confirmation."

Skye kept quiet then, conveying that it wasn't. Resigned not to push my luck, I didn't say anything else as I found a fallen log in decent shape to sit on. Neverland remained still around me, but the soft breezes rustling the trees sounded like a hundred sobbing voices. It prickled my skin and raised the hair on my arms.

Minutes passed.

My hands grew clammy. The longer Bay was gone, the more I twisted to look at the monolith, hoping he'd materialize out of the shadows. The longer he was gone, the more my hope waned that he would return at all.

"It's been ten minutes, hasn't it?" I whispered.

"It's been nearly thirty." Skye kicked his legs against my shoulder and wrung his hands in his lap. For a pixie, he had to be one of the calmest I'd seen. But since I couldn't understand them until recently, I hadn't made a point of getting to know many personally.

I gnawed my lip, letting out a breath. "I hope he's okay. Should we follow him…?"

Skye went still, his eyes bulging. Darting off my shoulder, he whirled beside me to face the structure. "That *bastard*!"

My mouth fell open. I snapped it shut as quickly as possible, lucky Skye's boiling focus was hyper-set on the temple. The tiny pixie people with bright hair and flower petal clothes *cursed*? Maybe Skye was special—he did spend all his time with Bay after all—but still.

It broke every innocent image I had of the creatures.

And I wasn't completely sure how not to respond to him for a few moments. Blinking out of the shock, I asked, "What is it?" A spike of terror shot through my gut, and I leaped to my feet. "Is Bay okay?"

Skye's nose scrunched in a sneer that made him look part feral dog. "I don't know," he growled. Facing me, he offered the non-verbal response of an infuriated shrug.

"Should we go in after him?" Anything could have happened. Thirty minutes was a long time, and I'd managed to nearly kill myself twice in less.

Skye shook his head, chiming, "No. You stay here." He motioned for me to wait, then zipped toward the entrance.

I jolted after him. "I'm not letting you go in there alone."

Skye froze, shooting me a glare.

I held my ground, planting my hands on my hips. "If something did happen, the last thing we want is for all of us to be separated. If you go alone and don't come back, I'll follow you, but I won't be able to fly. Our best chance is together."

He turned to look at the temple, then he faced me again. A sound I'd never expected to escape a pixie rumbled up his throat as he dredged his hands back through his hair. "Fine," he snapped. "Fine, you're right, and you can't understand me—" Frustrated, he scrubbed a hand down his face. Zipping to me, he nodded.

I nodded back, trying not to dig too much into the anger and concern melded on his face. Was he worried about Bay or mad at him? I didn't have the luxury to ask, so I took a breath and stepped forward, entering the darkness.

It swallowed us whole.

One hand fixed on the wall, I slipped forward and downward, testing the ground before placing my full weight onto any step. No light touched within, the black chasm seeming to stretch on forever. "Bay?" I hissed. My voice echoed against the stone, returning to me in distorted waves. "What was he expecting to find here?"

"Clues, answers, hints. He's desperate. He's looking for anything." Skye's voice drifted from the emptiness.

Answers to what questions? I pursed my lips, straining to pick the pixie's form out of the bleakness. The barest shimmer outlined him, but I couldn't make out his expression.

"This was a bad idea," I muttered. "We should turn around and make a torch or something before going deeper."

"Can't."

I hesitated, nearly asking why not, before shaking myself and remembering to act like I couldn't understand whether or not he'd agreed. Turning, I ran directly into a wall. "What?" I rubbed my nose and squinted, but naturally, I couldn't see the structure. I pressed my palm against the rough obstacle, fear curdling in my throat. "We can't get out."

"Nope."

My breaths shortened, and I halted on the step, scared to go forward unable to move back. It was so *dark*. "Where are you?" I asked, my voice more panicked than I would have liked.

A tiny sigh brushed near my ear, then little hands touched my forehead. The silkiest wisp of hair skimmed my skin as Skye pressed his head against mine. "I'm right here. Calm down. I'm not going to run off on my own, okay?" The soothing words turned harsh. "Unlike some people."

Gathering myself, I inhaled deeply, closed my eyes, and snapped them back open when I found no comfort in the action. There was absolutely no difference whether they were open or shut. "Can you see anything?" I whispered, adding, "Clap once for yes and twice for no.."

He clapped once, and my heart lifted before his voice fell on my ears again. "Well, I can see darkness, but that's hardly encouraging, so one clap for scared Lyric."

For the love of the airwoman, I was trapped in a temple with a sarcastic pixie. Acting like he could see enough to guide us forward would do no good, so I conceded to accept that desperate times called for profane language. "Damn it, Skye. If you can't see, don't pretend you can."

Silence.

I rolled my eyes, glad that at least I could feel his soft breath in front of me, entering and leaving his lungs. "Skye?"

"If you can understand me, clap once for yes and twice for no."

My teeth gritted. Out of spite, I clapped twice.

"Well." He moved, but his voice didn't go far. "Why have you pretended this entire time?"

"I haven't. I really couldn't understand you—or any of the others—last week."

Skye's tone morphed into the kind someone could only manage with folded arms and a look of condescension. "Then why have you pretended since last week?"

"Because," I spat, "Bay lies."

The pixie scoffed, muttering, "He sure does. Or did you actually believe all his stories?"

My cheeks flared red, and I was somewhat glad for the darkness in the moment. Putting that whole situation aside, I steered us back on topic. "That doesn't matter. What are we supposed to do?"

His wings buzzed in the darkness, flitting away before returning. "There's only one way to go, so let's continue down. There's a wind current in a few steps, so something must lie ahead, another exit. For all we know, Bay came this same way."

Carefully picking my way down the stone slabs, I sucked my finger and held it up. Just as Skye had said, a light breeze meandered from the right.

The more I focused on it, the stronger it became. The ground leveled, and I followed the wind around a corner.

"What does Bay need answers to so badly that he

would come in here alone? And why didn't you want to go with him?" The breeze whistled through the hall, growing stronger. I swore I could hear voices laced in it, murmurs and whispers, but when I tried to listen harder, the air rushed against me, whipping my hair and clothes back.

Skye slapped into my chest, clinging to my shirt, and I raised a hand to cover my eyes from the stinging onslaught. "What is this? It's unnatural!"

"A lot of things in Neverland are." Skye braced himself beneath my satchel strap like a belt.

The wind howled, as though in pain, so I yelled over it, "How can we be sure we're even going toward an exit then?"

"Do you have a better idea?"

I backstepped, but the phantom and silent wall blocking us from retreat met my back. There was only the one way to go. "No," I grumbled, pushing ahead. My hair beat against my neck and face, and I winced when the strands slashed at my eyes. "This would be so much easier if you would just *quiet down*!" I sliced my arm through the torrent, and wind wrapped around it like a physical sheet I could pull away, so I did.

Calm filled the tunnel, the gentle breeze returning to little more than an exhale of breath.

"What did you just..." Skye's chest heaved against my own.

I stood still, wondering the same. It couldn't have had anything to do with me. Not really. My brows furrowed when a glow blinked on in the distance. "Is that light?"

"Not sunlight."

I wasn't about to be picky. My pace quickened toward the blue-green hue. The closer I got, the larger the space around us became. The tunnel opened into a circular chamber illuminated by large flowers clinging to the ceiling. "Mirabel." The same flower that lit my room back in Skyla. My eyes searched the familiar petals and colors. "This is in Skyla, too."

"Sk-ye…is that you?" A fragmented voice trailed from one of many tunnels carved into the room before us. Something about it wasn't right.

Before I could say anything, Skye pushed away from me. "Bay."

"It hu-rts," the voice moaned, a breeze rustling from the same tunnel.

"Hold on!" Panic spiked in the pixie's tone.

"Wait!" I threw up my hand, but Skye had already darted into the tunnel. I started after him, colliding with a wall that slammed between us and blocked the path. "Skye!" I yelled, banging against the stone. "Skye, come back! Something isn't right. I don't think that's Bay!"

My nostrils flared, and my fists clenched. Teeth gritted, I rubbed my face. "I cannot keep running into walls," I grumbled, twisting to look at the other tunnels. A stone blocked the one we had come through, unsurprisingly. The rest were as dark and foreboding as everything else in this twisted place.

"Lyly."

Cold air poured from one of the tunnels, carrying a voice. Whisper's voice. My body stiffened against the chill.

"You should not be here," she said.

"I know that," I croaked. "I'm sorry. I never meant—"

"Trusting, innocent Lyly. You cannot trust anyone here." The voice aged, and hints of Tiger Lily melded into it. "Not even yourself."

"Are you a changeling?" I slipped my knife from its sheath on my thigh and brandished the blade. It caught the ghastly light, glinting floral reflections. "Your kind won't toy with me again."

"No." A woman whom I'd never heard before now spoke from the shadows, from the frigid wind. "I am the memory of my brothers and sisters, a wisp of magic manifested to guard our home, a kindred spirit. Come with me."

"But my friends—"

"Will be safe. Time is irrelevant here, but I shan't keep you for long." The woman's voice blended with others, hundreds, thousands, some vaguely familiar, the rest not. "We have been waiting. So long. So long in this timeless place. For the touch of another soul."

I gripped my knife, but the wind wrapped around me, beckoning me forward. "If I can't trust anyone, why should I trust you?"

"I am not anyone." The words came from behind, but only rock stood there. The voices floated on the breeze, coaxing, so I gave in.

There was little else I could do in a dark cave with no clear exit. Alone here now, my only hope of making it out and finding the others was to see where this led me and trust it was safe. *All things happen for a reason,* Tiger Lily had told me after her husband left. Tears had glistened in her eyes then, but she had continued to stare out at the sunset. *We may not know why, the pain may be unbearable, but if we trust ourselves and our hearts, we will find incredible things are born in our darkest moments.*

Peter, how come you don't age? Young, yet, I had looked up to him.

Sadness had crossed his brown eyes, but it lingered only for a second, then he ruffled my hair and grinned. *Maybe so I would have the chance to meet you.*

I couldn't explain a lot of things. I couldn't find reason in losing Whisper, leaving Peter, or following this voice. Still, as my feet continued to hit solid ground and I continued to breathe, I knew I had to keep moving forward. For everyone I still had, and for everyone I didn't.

"You cry," the wind murmured, touching the dampness on my cheeks.

Holding myself firm, I swallowed the lump in my throat. "If you aren't a someone, how can you see me?"

"Yes. And how can I speak?"

I froze. "My mind is playing tricks on me. You said I couldn't trust myself. What if you meant now, in following you?"

"Will you listen to me or not?" it hissed. "Taking what I say to do in part means nothing."

I didn't budge. "Why wouldn't I be able to trust myself then?"

"Because you know not what you are."

"I'm Lyric."

"And who is *Lyric*? The words drifting in the song of the air? The music on the wind? A charm of good fortune? A girl, a friend, a wanderer, an orphan?" The chill bit at my nose and fingers and ears. "You have always doubted you were anything. Because you knew, deep in your heart, you were nothing worth keeping."

My knife shook in my hand. "That's not true. Maybe —" I spat, "maybe I was abandoned, but the people who took me in, they kept me. And they're extraordinary. If I really am nothing and if I came from nothing special, then that means incredible people still saw something worthwhile in me." *And didn't that make me, just a little, incredible, too?* "I don't need your help. I'm going to trust myself here."

Long, icy fingers caressed my cheeks, and a breath escaped me. "Very well." Whisper's voice. I closed my eyes tight, wishing the wraith had picked anyone else. "We will meet again."

"I said I—" My eyes opened on a room illuminated by fire. Large sconces flickered with heat, painting the stone walls in orange. No tunnels led in or out of the space. I stood in the middle, staring ahead at pictures. Children's pictures.

Drawn into the wall in shades of sky blue and sun yellow and grass green and blood red were images depicting a stream of events. A lightning bolt struck what appeared to be a large rock—an island?—splitting it into dozens of fractured pieces. The pieces fell into the ocean and took root there. I stilled at seeing the next image.

It was a boy. A boy with burning hair, green clothes, and a splash of yellow gleaming near his shoulder. My fingers brushed over the stone. "Peter…?" The chipped paint had been there for years, maybe centuries. I couldn't tell. But I had always speculated Peter had existed for just as long.

The story continued. The boy traveled the islands, unraveling secrets that led him to a spring. At least it looked like a spring. This water, unlike the rest in the images, was a striking shade of gold, and he drank it.

The rest of the pictures were of forts and treehouses and swimming with mermaids and flying with birds. Casual child scribbles. The more I looked, the more seemed to appear, and the longer I tried to focus on any one in particular, the more convoluted they all became. Some of the pictures felt like stories I'd heard before. Others were crusted with time and lost to the ages.

The pictures spun in my head now more than on the walls, and I saw other children with the flame-haired boy. Several others. More that I recognized. A hook chipped them away until I knew each figure's name.

The Lost Boys.

The Lost Boys and Peter.

With that realization, wind appeared out of nowhere, crashing into me and throwing me off my feet. I hit stone. The impact jarred every thought and image, shaking them from my head. Sweat beaded on my brow in the firelight, then froze. Icelets flecked off my cheeks. An eerie voice called to me.

Then silence and darkness swallowed my mind.

"I can't believe you did this. She could have died."

"But, she didn't."

"We don't know that yet."

Someone slapped my cheeks. "Yes. We do," Bay growled. "She's fine."

I took a quivering breath, wondering how "fine" I

looked. It felt like I'd been put through a rock grinder and tumbled around with stones twice my size. Unfortunately, I couldn't quite find the strength to open my eyes.

"See? She's breathing."

"I know someone else who's breathing and not at all fine," Skye hissed.

Bay's hand rested on my cheek an instant before drawing away. "That's too far."

"*This* was too far." A light body landed on my shoulder. "I mean it, Bay. No one else suffers for our family. No one."

I had to pry myself awake. Were we still in the cave? Was that sunlight or firelight against my face?

Taking a heaving breath, I cracked open my eyelids and squinted through the trees at the dying sun. Bay sighed over me, smiling. "Hello, Wind Song. Are you back with us?"

Sand coated my tongue. Everything ached. Was I meant to always be in a state of pain here?

"Wa-ter?" I croaked.

Bay's eyes widened. "Water? What about—"

"She wants water, you idiot." Skye darted off my shoulder and dove into Bay's bag, pulling a flask larger than him out when he emerged.

"Right," Bay mumbled, taking the weight from Skye and propping my head so I could drink. The liquid washed down my throat, cooling my chest and lightening the strain on my breath. When I'd had enough, I could almost sit up on my own.

"What…happened?" I remembered the voice in the wind and the pictures. Was either real? Now, looking back and finding myself inexplicably here, a haze covered it all, like I was peering into a dream.

"I'm not sure. We woke up here shortly before you did."

"So does this feeling like death thing wear off fairly quickly, or am I just special?" Flexing my fingers and toes, I tested whether or not I could move my limbs. Not well, apparently, but some.

"I, uh…" Bay met Skye's glare as the tiny creature hovered defensively before me. "I think you're just special."

"Lovely." I glanced at the space around me, realizing that though it was quiet, the stale air from before had lessened. "Where are we?" A large cylindrical building sat surrounded by blazing orange flowers. Unlike the other homes, this one appeared mostly intact. Yet two gravestones jutted out of the flowers, proving the battle hadn't left even here unscathed.

Bay turned toward the solemn home, and his jaw clenched. Sorrow saturated his gaze, but he wiped the expression clean when he looked back at me. "This is where the former chief lived with his family." Rising, he held a hand out for me, helping me onto my feet. "We should probably take shelter here for the night."

"What?" I snatched my hand out of his, regretting it when the world toppled. He steadied me, nothing but concern in his hazel eyes. I swallowed a shaking breath and forced myself to remain calm, if for no reason other than the headache brewing. "Wouldn't that be disrespectful?"

His attention shifted to the graves. "I don't think they would mind…and I don't think you'd make it to my next shelter. Not right now, anyway. It's probably better if we don't hobble through the night."

"I'm not hobbling."

"You're right," Skye snipped. "You're not even hobbling. Come on. It's fine." He motioned me forward, raising his brows at Bay.

Bay cleared his throat. "He says it's fine also."

I glanced between them. Had I dreamed the pixie finding out I could understand him? Or was he respecting my reasons for not telling Bay in the first place? It didn't matter right now. Protection from the night and possibly a place to sleep took precedence. "Fine." I stared at the doorway, trying to keep my focus off the graves. "If you're sure."

Skye nodded and zipped ahead through the cracked door while Bay eased me forward, one step at a time. "Whatever happened really did a number on you," he said close to my ear. "Do you…remember anything?"

A little too much hope laced his voice as if he knew something had happened, and though it had left me unable to walk, he wanted to know what it was. Shaking my head, I mumbled, "Nothing I can remember. It was dark."

"Right." The frail hope dissipated, planting a seed of guilt in my chest.

He had lied to me more than once—I was half certain he had planned this whole event too; for some reason I couldn't discern. Why should I feel bad about keeping information I didn't understand from him? Glancing at his face, seeing the absence of any gleam in his eye, I figured out why.

He's desperate.

If I hadn't imagined everything with Skye, Bay was just as he'd said—*desperate*. Perhaps the answers or hints or clues he was looking for had poured into my head through those pictures, but until I knew what they meant and the reason he was looking for them, I didn't feel comfortable sharing.

I dropped my attention to the bed of flowers just before the front door. They blazed in the last rays of light, each spotted orange lily bursting with new life in the desolate area. Bobbing in the breeze, they radiated a sense of calm I hadn't felt since…

"Tiger lilies." Bay nudged the door open fully with his foot, meeting my gaze when I looked up.

My throat tightened in on itself, but I managed a whispered, "What?"

He nodded at the patch of flowers. "They're tiger lilies. The chief's wife planted them here to honor their daughter's birth in the time of peace before the slaughter."

Without another word, my gaze still fixed on the brilliant blooms, Bay pulled me inside.

15TH NOVEMBER

As we walked through the deepest part of the forest we had come upon yet, I could hardly keep my attention on the still-dull ache tracing down my limbs. A weight held me to the earth even though dust coated my hair and skin. Bay floated beside me, oblivious.

Could the tiger lilies in front of the chief's house be a coincidence?

The images of Peter plastered against the stone walls of that temple cave made me think otherwise. If Peter had been here, perhaps Tiger Lily had been too. Perhaps, this was even her original home. It all tied together. Hook, enemy of the natives and Peter. Peter, enemy of Hook and friend of most. Tiger Lily, Peter's oldest living friend—as far as I knew.

What if there had been more Lost Boys? What if Hook had vanquished them? What if Peter had saved a chieftain's daughter and escaped to Skyla with the ones he had left?

What if Bay, all this time, knew the truth? What if he had the entire story, the one Peter had long since forgotten, and I suppose Tiger Lily was either too young to remember or chose not to share?

"You're awfully quiet this morning." Bay didn't smile. The solemn tastes from the day before lingered, but more than that, he appeared on edge. A bird streaked overhead with a splitting caw, and the fearless boy who laughed casually in the face of Krakens stiffened, watching the feathered fiend disappear into the distance before daring to relax.

"I guess I don't feel much like talking." The half-lie spilled easily from my lips, exhaustion a dark cloud clinging to me like a tick. I wanted desperately to talk about all the questions and speculations spinning in my head. But I couldn't shake the feeling that what the voice in the wind had said before was the truth. I couldn't trust anything here. Not Bay. Not Skye. Not even myself—seeing as my first instinct was to blurt everything to him and wait for answers I doubted would come. That last bit was hardly new. Since when did I trust myself anyway?

Grief pooled in my veins, making me something pliable and reliant, but there was nothing to rely on—everything I had once relied on was little more than a ghost to haunt me now. I was here for revenge and bloodshed, so no wonder Neverland wasn't making it easy for me. The magical island had seen far too much of both.

Bay rebraided his hair and tightened the tie around the short tail. "Are you reluctant to talk because of yesterday?"

A nerve snapped. "Which part of yesterday? Leading me through piles of bones or tricking me into following you through a sacred temple?"

"I didn't trick you?" His eyes widened with innocence. "I said I had to go. You just happened to follow me."

"You knew I would." I trudged on, pushing aside a low-hanging branch. "Don't act like you didn't have it planned from the start. I just can't figure out why. We both could have *died*."

Bay landed beside me, his bare feet squishing through damp clumps of leaves, and I caught him glance accusingly at Skye.

I snapped, "No, your pixie didn't mime the truth to me. Maybe I'm just a little smarter than you thought."

"I've never thought you weren't smart." He frowned. "I wouldn't have invited dead weight to come with me to a place as deadly as this. I don't have time to babysit, Wind Song."

Stopping, I whirled on him and placed my hands on my hips. He stopped just short of running into me, and I hovered half an inch taller than him, just like Peter often did to me. "Then, I want the truth. What do you know about Peter and Tiger Lily? How are they connected to this place? Am I?"

His lips parted, then they closed. His eyes drifted toward the ground, then a bird screamed near us, and he jerked. "Shit!" Fear curdled in his eyes as he peered through the thick forest for the offending creature.

"While we're at it, why don't you tell me why birds are scaring you out of your skin today?" I settled back on the ground and folded my arms, forcing my attention to remain steady on him instead of traveling through the trees, looking for danger. He knew this place. If he was scared of something, I would likely be terrified. But I didn't have that luxury right now.

He swiped his bangs back and glared at me. "Fine. You want me to confirm it? Tiger Lily was the chief's daughter. Thanks to Peter, she was the only native who hadn't already left who escaped the slaughter."

My mouth went dry. "So...this all couldn't have happened more than twenty years ago."

"Ninteen." Bay's eyes closed, and he took a deep breath. "It happened about nineteen years ago."

I looked at Bay, seeing the soft lines near his eyes. He looked like a boy, only two years older than I was. But when his hazel gaze fixed on me, I saw wisdom in his eyes. "You... Were you there?" I asked.

A self-degrading smile tipped his lips. "What do you think, Wind Song?"

I didn't know what to think. I didn't have time to respond either. Something white and brown screamed through the trees behind Bay, and Skye shrieked, "Run!"

Our feet pounded against the ground, each thudding step reminding me of the aches and pains I had encountered the day before. My muscles tightened from the strain, each tendon one jarring pull away from snapping.

The trees were packed together like woven threads, impossible to maneuver through quickly by air. So, we continued running, listening to the branches behind us catch wings and flailing limbs. Bay mumbled curses beneath his breath and threw glances in my direction to make sure I kept up. We gained ground for a moment.

Then my foot caught on a fallen log. I careened into the brush, my flesh shredded on the harsh bark. My ankle burned, and I hissed, clutching it with both hands.

"Wind Song, get up!" Bay gripped my shoulder, yanking me back onto protesting feet. A sharp stab shot through my calf. Sweat poured into my cut and stung. I forgot how to breathe for a moment, then I gasped in air, my eyes watering.

Staring ahead, I met the huge eyes of an owl. The creature's beak split in a deafening trill, and I blurted, "That's not a siren!"

"Nope! It's a harpy!" Bay grabbed my hand and ripped me away from the half-human half-bird abomination. Unlike the sirens who could pass as beautiful and graceful, this creature appeared made of mismatched parts, awkwardly battling through the trees.

"What in the name of the airwoman is a harpy?" I screamed, fighting to keep my legs moving. The surety I would die if I stopped was all the motivation I needed to fight through every rattling step.

"*That* is a harpy." Bay squeezed my hand, tugging me through a narrow gap between two towering spruce trees, and my mouth fell open.

"Is *that* why you've been scared of birds today?"

"I haven't been scared of birds," he protested.

The screeching harpy yowled in pain, and I dared a look back to find its wing trapped on a branch. "So normal people who aren't scared of birds panic whenever one tweets in their vicinity?"

Bay dodged a thorny bush. "Okay, fine. But who likes birds anyway?"

"I do. I mean, I *used* to!"

"We're almost there!" Skye chirped.

"Great." Bay tossed his hair back, peered over his shoulder at the harpy, and released a breath. "I think we're going to make it."

"What? Make it where?"

"Just trust me."

I was told explicitly not to, and all signs pointed to that being a good idea, but I didn't quite have a choice right now—worse yet, I still wanted to trust him. The forest broke suddenly, displaying a sheer cliff. Bay pulled me over the edge, and we plummeted.

Water spilled from the rock at more than a dozen points, each waterfall distinct as it rushed into snaking streams at the bottom. Mist sprayed my body, soaking me to the skin.

"Hold your breath!" Bay yelled.

No sooner than I'd taken a gasping breath did he plunge us through the falls. Any hope of flying washed off in the downpour, and we rolled in a pile of appendages across a stone floor. I panted once the world stopped spinning.

Bay dragged himself into a seated position and rubbed his neck. "Well, that was eventful."

The rushing water before us muted anything beyond, but I still jumped when a distant caw broke through the full silence. Shivering, I tried adjusting myself to stand, but the scrape on my ankle wasn't having it, so I slumped. "Everything hurts. Again." Out of habit, I felt for my bag—wet, also again, and my knife. It was all still here.

A sharp breath whistled through my nose when Bay grabbed my ankle and stretched out my leg. He examined the purple area then pressed on my heel, watching me for any reaction. Shifting his bag in front of him, he set my foot down. "It's not broken or sprained, thankfully." He pulled out a damp roll of scrap cloth and wrung out what water he could before using it to clean and wrap my cut. "Another bruise for your collection."

I grimaced at his grin and pulled my treated leg close against my chest. "I'm glad it amuses you."

"I've never met someone so attracted to danger before."

Grumbling, I said, "I think it's attracted to me."

"So I have a rival. We might as well stop here for a soggy lunch." Bay fished out some food from his bag, half of it unappetizing, yet my stomach growled in response. He passed me the better pieces of tough bread and a handful of berries. "We aren't far from Pirate Bay now. We'll reach my base tonight, and then it's just a short walk through the meadow come morning."

"Wonderful."

His gaze flicked up, and he watched me for a long moment. "You're welcome to stay in my base for as long as you need to plan your attack."

"I'll scout everything out as soon as possible." Tearing off a piece of bread, I popped it in my mouth and avoided dwelling on the mushy texture. I was almost there. Almost to what was sure to be my demise. The most I could do was attempt to thin the adversary, then hopefully, Skyla would have a better chance.

"Your best chance is probably to light it up," Bay murmured. "I know where the explosives are kept. Gunpowder. Lighting fuel. It might take a bit of strategy, but if you can set the bay on fire, you'll be able to wipe it off Neverland before anyone would notice."

I stared at him, eyes wide. "I thought you couldn't enter in case someone recognized you?"

Popping a berry in his mouth, he shrugged. "Yeah, if someone recognizes me, it's all over, but I guess I've changed my mind about how much I'm willing to help you. If I can help it, I'm not sending you to your death."

I dropped my gaze to the bandage around my ankle. Like the others, it had been wrapped with precision and habit. How many wounds had he suffered in the years he'd spent here? How long had it been just him and Skye looking for something always out of reach? "Thank you," I whispered, and before I realized, I added, "If I survive this, maybe I can help you next."

"You wouldn't want to go home?" Softness blanketed the question because we both knew that's exactly what I wanted, especially right now when everything hurt. It's probably all either of us wanted: *to go home*. He was really asking why I felt I didn't have that option anymore.

I stuffed several berries in my mouth, downed the sweet-bitter flavor, and swallowed. "Peter forgets things. The kinds of things you don't think you can ever forget. It doesn't take long. He's never mourned anything. He just…forgets any reason he might have to be sad."

"You think he's forgotten you."

I nodded. "And with Whisper and Tiger Lily…"

"Right," he said as Skye settled on his shoulder. He looked at the silent creature. "I'm sorry. I didn't mean to… Well…, yeah."

My lips pulled in a twisted grin. "Very smooth, Star Boy."

He met my expression with a pained smile of his own. "I do try, Wind Song. I do try."

We finished our pathetic meal before launching ourselves out of the crevice and catching fresh pixie dust to avoid an untimely collision with the ground. Landing among sparse trees and winding streams, we maintained a slow pace as every step stung or ached or stabbed somewhere new in me.

I planted my focus around me as completely as I could to avoid dwelling on the pain rushing my body in overwhelming tides. The area was beautiful. Color saturated the banks of each stream, hundreds of flowers and butterflies painting everything in a rainbow kaleidoscope. Perfumed scents rose and fell on the wind as it rustled the slender trees, their light branches swaying.

If my head wasn't throbbing, I might have enjoyed it.

"Here we are," Bay stopped, and I looked up from a cluster of yellow buds dancing in the breeze.

A wide span of meadow stretched before us. The streams pooled together in a rushing river that skittered off to one side and plowed toward the ocean that glinted on the horizon. Bobbing atop what blue waves I could see were massive ships, each and every one bearing some form of black or red flag. The ocean I couldn't see was blocked by a town with a variety of square buildings. Some jutted into the sky. Others sat squat near the ground. No two shapes appeared entirely the same. They rested in blocks like a clump of fool's gold.

My nose scrunched when some acrid fume reached me. "What is that?"

"Cheap rum." Bay tilted his head toward the setting sun. "At this time, barrels and barrels of cheap rum."

"It's awful." I covered my mouth to avoid heaving.

Shadows coated Bay's eyes when the sun dipped completely from view, leaving nothing but a faint glow in the sky. "You get used to it," he said, the words dark. Jaw clenched, he sighed. "I suppose we have some work to do tonight. No offense, but you don't look particularly pirate-y." He brushed some crawling flowers off a trap door at the base of several slender trees. Bound together, the trunks hid the secret chamber well from view. "It might be a bit of a mess. It's been a while since I've come here."

I stared into the dim hole and shook my head. "That's all right. I doubt it's worse than what we've already gone through today." *Beside*—I sank into the cool embrace of the earth, my breath catching when I found mirabel decorating the ceiling—*it's practically home.*

"I look like a milkmaid," I grumbled, staring at my reflection in the slim mirror propped against the dirt walls of Bay's hideout. As he'd said, everything was a bit dusty, and we had fought several webs away, but it remained the closest thing to home I'd come across since entering Neverland.

Bay floated behind me, his chin propped in his palm. "Yeah, yeah, you kind of do."

I swiped the rag off my head, freeing my hair, and hovered to avoid putting pressure on my bruised ankle. My orange locks spilled into my eyes, so I blew them away. "Don't other people have orange hair? Surely Peter isn't the only one, and I'm not even blood-related to him, so he absolutely isn't."

"Maybe, but no one here that I remember. It isn't every day Neverland has visitors, so we really need to blend in. It's bad enough I can't do anything about that gold in your eyes." Bay turned toward the chest of attire we were picking apart and dug deeper.

I faced the mirror again, staring at the golden rings around my irises. A phantom brush of wind that couldn't have come from anywhere down here teased the candle resting on a table to my left, and I lowered my brows at it.

"How about this!" Bay wrenched my attention away from the flame and toward the cotton dress in his hand. Some kind of laced and leather contraption rested in his other palm, and he waved it. "It comes with a thing."

I took the tangled mess from him and frowned. "I think this is a corset."

"Try it on."

"Um. No." I returned it to him. "I already have clothes." I gestured at my trousers and leather vest over a white top. "We need to figure out the hair problem." Planking above the trunk midair, I tried to find a better bandana than the one that made me look like I'd come straight from the goat farms. Instead, I found a small woven bag with long needles and a glass jar of ink. "What's this?"

Bay dumped the rejected outfit and peered over my shoulder. "A tattoo kit." Reaching for it, he stopped, and his hand clenched in a fist. "A friend taught me long ago."

I turned the bag over, examining the faded dye coloring the wool. "This looks like something Tiger Lily would make."

"I'd imagine so. Her mother made it."

My heart dropped into my stomach and stuck there. "What?"

"Receiving a mark was a tradition when children came of age. Generally, the mark represented some achievement or title.. Usually, it tied in with the child's name since the native's names tended to change with either of those things. Her father taught me. Her mother made me a set of my own." Scoffing, he ran his fingers through his loose hair. "What were they thinking? I was —what?—maybe ten?" His voice quieted. "Though, I suppose not technically… Anyway, I never really got to use it on anything past animal hide. They said when Tiger Lily came of age, I'd be the one honored to do her mark, but…that didn't happen either."

Running my finger along the spine of a bone needle, I whispered, "What's of age?"

"Sixteen."

Pressing my lips together, I lowered myself onto the rug and sat cross-legged, handing him the set of needles and ink. "Then, I guess we're both a little late."

His brows rose, and he blinked. "What?"

"Tiger Lily was more like a mother to me than

anyone. If she was the last of her people and this tradition died with her, without her even knowing, I couldn't bear it. You seem to know what you're talking about, so tell me and show me. Let me keep some of my mother's heritage alive." I kept my eyes fixed on him, and gradually he sat across from me, taking the tools and holding them tight.

"It doesn't go away."

I provided him an annoyed glare. "I do know what a tattoo is."

He wet his lips. "I mean, it's been a while since I learned. Any mistakes won't go away."

"Then don't make any."

He laughed, but I raised my brows, and he quieted. Glancing around the room, he found Skye asleep on a pillow in the corner. "You must have some insane faith in me."

I looked him over, from his tousled waves to his bare feet. Even "seated," he floated slightly above the ground. Sincerity, memories, and honor for a culture he had touched weighted his expression. I took a breath. "Is that a mistake?"

He nodded. "Probably."

And yet right now, it didn't feel like it was. "Will you be honest with me, Bay?"

"If I can." He looked back at me, as though he was waiting for a question, but I had already asked it, and his reply was about as good as I was going to get.

I held out my arms, unsure what the next step was.

He smiled, shaking his head. "It's going to be a later night than I expected."

16TH NOVEMBER

Overnight, my right arm had gone red around the markings, but the pictures remained clear. Half a dozen tiny feathers floated down my skin like a breeze chased them.

They were perfect, and when I asked why Bay had chosen them over music notes or something relating to "Wind Song,", hed merely shrugged and said he couldn't help it; they were from my wings. *Wings,* I thought, resting at the base of the cluster of trees and staring out at the dozens of butterflies playing by the stream banks. If I had wings like them, where would I go? If I didn't need dust or a friendly pixie near me, if I could be as independent and strong as Whisper, what would I do?

I probably wouldn't have run away to Neverland with a death wish.

Releasing a breath, I glanced back down at my sleeve of feathers, then stretched my hand to the sky. Sunlight poured through my fingers and over the designs.

"It's there for good," Bay said, emerging from the trap

door with Skye and stretching in the air. A yawn clung to his mouth, so he covered it with a hand, mumbling through it, "I hope you aren't having regrets. I'd feel terrible if I spent seven hours on something you'd regret."

His expression made me think it wouldn't bother him in the slightest. I dropped my arm back into my lap. "I love it."

"Good." He smirked, fluttering an orange bandana at me. "I found this for your hair. Maybe no one will notice if a bit peeks through."

"Are we leaving now, then?" I tied the cloth around my head, hoping it looked normal enough, and stood.

Leaning forward, Bay provided me a once-over that ended with him tucking an already-straying lock of hair back beneath the cloth. My cheeks heated, but he moved away without reacting. "Almost. What do you think?" Plucking a dark eye mask from his darker coat, he covered half his face, not the half that showcased a carefree grin, though.

"Little too friendly and floaty for a pirate if you ask me."

His smile fell as he planted his feet on the ground. "Good thing you're beat up enough for the both of us if I'm too 'friendly,'" Shaking his hair out, he brushed off his cloak, mumbling something about how Skye shed worse than a cat.

Skye shot me a warning look and an eye roll. I held in a laugh.

"All right. That's that," he stated, resting his arm on the hilt of his cutlass. His usual dagger belt remained in place, but the cutlass definitely added a much-needed pirate-y flare. "Let's hope we survive this. We've both got things to do afterward."

"I suppose when we get to those things, you'll finally tell me what they are?"

"Surprise is the spice of life." Lifting his coat, he let Skye zip into an inner pocket, then we began walking.

"Are we talking surprise like: 'Surprise! It's your birthday!' or surprise like 'Surprise! A harpy is chasing you through the woods, and the only chance of surviving you have is jumping off a cliff and diving through a waterfall at the exact moment a ledge is hidden behind it'?"

"Closer to the second one, but with sprinkles."

"Lovely." My smile betrayed the subtle anxiety swirling in my chest. I felt lighter today, even with the task looming before me. We had to hunt down Hook and his crew, and wipe them from Neverland before they could ever reach Skyla, yet it was less daunting beside Bay. He may be a liar, and I might not know much about him—he may have even intentionally put me in danger for undisclosed reasons—but he still gathered confidence around him like a living beast.

Beside him, impossible things felt probable. Win or lose, it was all a game, and he'd come out laughing in the end.

"You're a lot like Peter," I murmured.

His nose scrunched, and he stopped short. "What?"

"The way you act, fearlessly and all that. A bit cocky. Easily able to tread my nerves. Never providing enough information—though I'm pretty certain he can't, and you just choose not to." Perhaps pixies only ever clung to a very specific type of person—the most innocent assholes.

Bay deadpanned. "Thank you for comparing me to your father figure slash twelve-year-old somehow-your-guardian person. My pride is not at all wounded, and I am also not at all resentful."

"I don't think it's a bad thing. I've lived my entire life wishing I could be like Peter." A cloud drifted along the horizon, disappearing behind buildings and peeking through the cracks. "He's completely free."

Bay huffed a breath. "He is definitely not. He has all of Skyla to look after."

"Maybe, but he does it effortlessly like he's playing king. And, when he doesn't feel like it, he goes on an adventure, returning with any stories he remembers, making up the ones he doesn't." I frowned.

Bay laughed, but the sound was so bitter as he started walking again. "He has you completely tricked."

"What are you talking about?"

"Peter is anything but free. When he leaves, he's keeping up relations with all the other kingdoms that he has kept Skyla majorly outside of. His adventures are tasks at their cores, tasks that keep Skyla safe from the messes on the ground."

"How would you know?" I spat.

"Because I know Peter. Or rather I knew him, and when I knew him, it was in a time of war. Trust me, that perpetual kid lives in a constant cycle of duty and suffering."

My head shook of its own accord. "I don't want to hear this." My bright mood died, and my chest clenched. I knew Bay lied, it could all be a lie, but—

"Sorry…" Bay scrubbed a hand across his mouth. "Of course, you wouldn't. I guess the comparison hit a little close to home, is all."

"Is the way you see Peter how you see yourself?" I stilled on the edge of the town. Just a few more yards and we'd have to put any strange talk aside, and I had to know. What duties was he bound to that made him suffer?

"I'll never admit it." The dark air lifted, his hazel eyes gleaming within the mask. "After all, I'm nothing like that brat. Not even a little bit."

"I thought you said you'd be honest with me." Genuine hurt touched my heart, but I bit my cheek and pretended I was angry.

"When I can," he said. "Sometimes, it's too hard. Sometimes, I can't even be honest with myself." Before I could prod him further, he strode the rest of the way into the town, ducking into a dark alley. Hurrying after him was all I could do to keep up.

We kept to the shadows, trailing through alleyways until my head spun with every crooked path. When what seemed like an hour had passed, I caught Bay's coat and hissed, "I thought you knew where we were going?"

"Ah." He glanced back at me, his mask catching a straying streak of sunlight and sheening obsidian. "About that. We passed the storage forty minutes ago. They've changed things."

My mouth gaped. "How long has it been since you were last here?"

"A while, I told you that." His attention shifted to the street in front of us when a sturdy man flew across the alley's exit. A tall woman with golden teeth and brilliant raven hair leaped after him like a snarling cat. "Maybe we should go another way."

"Another way to where?" I asked as Bay backstepped toward me. He stopped in the narrower part of the walkway, his chest nearly pressed against mine. Masterly-crafted stone foundations made up the walls around us, but they were askew in their placement, acting like a funnel, a funnel that had sifted us closer than I would have liked.

"Just elsewhere. We're looking for something, so we need to keep looking, right?" A tinge of annoyance touched his tone, but his gaze remained off me and on the two people who were fighting.

I started to turn my gaze toward them when he caught my face with his hand, firmly shaking his head. A garbled cry mingled with shrieks of triumph, and I didn't need to see what had happened.

"You need to chill," Skye muttered from within Bay's coat, "and I need to breathe. Let's regroup at that place if it's still there."

My brows furrowed, wanting clarification more than translation. "What did he say?"

Bay narrowed his eyes on the mouth of the alley, then snatched my hand, ignoring everything he had just seen. "He says we need a break. I'm hungry. Are you hungry? Let's get some food."

Without an explanation, he pulled me along behind him through the narrow exit and into another—thankfully, wider—alley. We crossed it and two others before spilling out onto a cobblestone road. Here, something like laughter trickled on the breeze, kinder conversations spinning in the air. Bay towed me past a group of young women, and one smiled at me before resuming her conversation. "Are we still in Pirate Bay?" I mused.

"Hush." He squeezed my hand and dragged me up a gentle incline of stone slabs. His head bobbed from one side to the next, ever alert even though the grimy, dangerous place had changed into something almost peaceful.

I huffed but obliged to remain quiet.

When we crested the hill, a pocket of buildings stood before us, their doors open, letting scents of cooked food waft by. My mouth watered. It had been a week since I'd eaten properly cooked food. Was this safe?

Not to say much on Neverland seemed to be. It was easy enough to die standing still.

I, for one, was willing to take the risk.

We stepped into a building, a wash of scented heat coating my skin. I didn't even care if it came with a layer of grease that made my flesh want to crawl. All I could think about was a warm meal.

"Table for two?" a woman droned from behind an upright barrel, serving as a waiter's stand. She tapped a pen against the sheet of parchment laid across it and regarded us with tired eyes. Her gaze flicked between us a couple times, but no lights went off.

"A private room, actually," Bay responded, his tone mimicking hers, flawlessly bored.

I looked up at him, impressed.

The woman's lips contorted with something like a smile, and she folded her arms atop the barrel, adjusting her weight and pressing a heavy bosom against them. "That's sweet, kid, but probably a little outta your price range. What? You new here? Just wash up on shore?"

Bay's responding sigh was likewise impressive in the you-dare-insult-me area. In a single smooth motion, he reached into his coat and drew out a bag, tossing it before her. It clinked with the weight of many gold coins. "Quite the opposite, dear. Don't bother getting up. I know the way."

Leaving the woman with wide eyes, he snatched my hand again and pulled me through an arrangement of tables in an open room. Each patron appeared consumed in their own food or in their company, too bothered to glance up, so we cleared them without event.

In the back, we traversed a hall. Thick gauze and silk was pulled back from each of several doorways. Bay walked into one room and dropped the curtains as he did. Inside, a round table with a cushioned booth circling it rested on polished wooden floor before two gauze-covered windows. Two sheets of paper I assumed were the menus lay on the table on either side of a half-melted candle. It's firelight flickered, spilling shadows over the walls.

"Is this the lap of luxury?" I whistled when Bay released my hand.

He plopped into one side of the booth, lifted his coat flap, and stared at me, unanswering.

Skye zipped free immediately, darting about the room like a hummingbird. I watched him for a moment, my patience thin. Bay's attitude today had been nothing short of shitty. Dropping into the least graceful curtsy anyone could ever make, I pinned him with a glare. "Sorry, may I speak now, Your Highness? Or would you prefer I remain hushed?"

Lifting a menu, he murmured, "You can speak now."

I flinched. Stomping over to the seat across from him, I plopped against the cushion, forcing myself not to sigh into the plushness. "That wasn't actually a question. What's wrong with you today?"

Skye smacked into my shoulder and clung to the cloth of my shirt. "We're surrounded by a lot of people who want to kill him. He's seen a lot of old faces in one afternoon, and none of them are friendly. Well, anymore."

Bay's eyes narrowed on Skye before he snapped, "Nothing." Flailing a hand at me, he said, "Pick whatever you want to eat. I've got the doubloons to cover it."

Skye squeezed my shirt, so I swallowed my retort, snatched the menu, and repeated, "*Doubloons*." What a weird-ass word. Scowling at the print, I hardly realized when Skye vanished from sight, and a woman entered the room.

Significantly more cheerful than the lady at the front, she smiled at us, displaying a missing tooth. Her nose hooked at the halfway point, like it had been broken awkwardly once, and I couldn't help but think the freckled brunette didn't seem the fighting type. "Hello! My name's Taffy, and I'll be taking care of you today. Can I help you both to some drinks, and are you ready to order, or should I give you a few minutes?"

"We'll need a few minutes," Bay answered, "but two rum and waters will work to start."

"Two rum and waters, great. Take all the time you

need." She shot us another smile before leaving the room.

"Rum?" I sneered, as though Taffy could still hear us beyond the gauze.

"I'll drink yours. You can have the water."

My brows jumped. "So, you're getting drunk now?"

"It's decently watered down. The supply and demand around here is a little out of kilter." He lowered the menu and peered at me over the flickering candle. In that moment, his eyes appeared weary and cruel. "This isn't anything new to me, and I know what I'm doing. A little trust would be nice since I'm risking my neck here."

A bitter taste coated my tongue and contorted my insides until my chest clenched. "I never asked you to, so if you're just going to be one massive asshole, you can get lost, Star Boy. I'll figure this out on my own."

Skye appeared once more, settling on Bay's shoulder this time. *"This is where you apologize, asshole."*

Bay's jaw clenched, and he shifted his gaze back down. Mumbling, he capitulated. "You'd die." Then softer, "I can't let you die."

Skye sighed, sending me a shrug that meant "I tried."

Something was going on. Something more than I could see. That much was clear. But little else was. Taffy returned with our drinks, and the scent of the rum made my nose scrunch. Bay asked for more time, and we were alone again, glaring at our menus like they'd killed our firstborns.

"Why not?" I asked after deciding I wanted a turkey leg and fried onions—I don't think I ever wanted anything more than a turkey leg and fried onions.

Bay didn't look up. "What?"

"Why can't you let me die?" Setting my menu aside, I stared at him.

He didn't provide the same courtesy. "It's not obvious?"

"Not really."

"Sorry," he began, but it wasn't really an apology, "my mistake. I thought we were friends."

The notion may have been sweet had a thick layer of sarcasm not coated each syllable as thickly as the layer of grease on my skin. I snapped, "So?"

His menu hit the table harder than I would have thought possible. He clenched my gaze with his eyes and didn't waver in the hold. "Friends care about friends. You don't let people you care about just die."

His words hit like a knife thrown into my gut. I couldn't breathe for a second, but gasped when I remembered why. That's exactly what I'd done. I clutched a feather painted on my right arm and squeezed till my skin burned.

"Wake up, idiot," Skye hissed from somewhere.

Realization fell over Bay's face, but the damage had been done. I glanced at the gauzy exit and was on my feet. Bay caught my hand before I made it far.

"Let go of me!" I demanded. A breeze rushed from nowhere and squelched the candle, dimming the light in the room to whatever made it through the covered windows. Tears welled in my eyes, blurring his face and that stupid mask that made him someone I didn't know.

"No." He held on tighter, daring to pull my body against his. Heat erupted where flesh met flesh, but I accounted it all to anger. "I'm sorry. You know I didn't… I didn't mean anything by that. I care about you."

"Shut up."

"I don't think I will, Wind Song. I care about you. That's all I meant."

Gauze rustled behind me, and Bay looked up for an instant, his demeanour flicking into something else for a split second. The gauze rustled again, and that character switched back off. Tenderness encompassed his touch as he caressed my cheek with his free hand and dropped his attention back to my eyes.

"I'm going to hit you," I stated, less forcefully than I wanted.

He shrugged, his chest rubbing against mine. "I'd deserve it."

Everything had changed the moment we stepped into this bay, and it was more than the threat presented. I wasn't an idiot. People like Bay and Peter got a high off threats. The challenge was welcome. He'd laughed at the Kraken and grinned when we'd plummeted over the cliff away from the harpy. What was a town full of pirates to him but a maze with consequences? "Are you going to tell me exactly what's wrong with you?"

He plopped his forehead against mine. "I'm an asshole."

"Yeah, besides that."

His eyes went half-lidded, and even so close, he looked away. Before he replied, I knew his answer wouldn't be one at all. "I'm the prince of the assholes."

Closing my eyes, I dwelled on his hold around my wrist a little too heavily. Would I ever get to know him like I wanted? Or was I just another game? He was all I had left, but I wasn't something so precious. I was hardly anything at all. Throat tight, I whispered, "You're the damn king."

He chuckled, "Sadly, no," but wouldn't elaborate.

The sun dipped out of sight, and I sighed, glancing at Bay. He rested against the alley wall, his lips pinched in thought. "Well?" I asked.

"A lot has changed. A lot more than I thought." His mouth opened again, but he shut it before letting anything else escape.

"Do we head back and try again in the morning?" Rambling, singing, and drunken shouts grew with every minute. The darker it got, the lighter the voices, the more violence coiled around the bay.

He stiffened. "I don't know if we'd make it back without suspicion. It's normal for pirates to leave for a time and return, but hardly anyone has a base in the wild. This place, however filthy, is home. If anyone saw us come and go and they see us again in the morning, we may attract the worst kind of attention."

I laughed. "Which would be?"

"Hook's." He stuffed his hands in his coat pockets, balling them into fists. "Here, he's king. Nothing weird happens without going through him. He built his empire here ever since he failed against Pan, and he rules with an iron hand."

"Literally." I smirked, but Bay only shot me a frown.

Sighing, he ran his fingers through his hair and leaned his head back to look at the sky. The navy hue bled out with every moment that passed; with every moment that passed, Bay's mask blended with the shadows until only his hazel eyes caught slips of stray light. "We'll have to get a place here for the night."

"Will that be as simple as getting dinner?"

His eyes closed, disappearing from view into the shadows of his mask. "I've never actually done it before. I'm not sure I even know where to start. Nights tend to be late here, too." He dragged one hand from his pocket and rubbed his mouth. Exhaustion filtered off him in waves. "I hate this place."

My heart sank, and I had to remind myself I never asked him to help me this much. I never asked him to enter this place. If he hadn't already decided to take me this far by the time we landed, all I would have asked for would have been a map. I'd likely have been some strange thing's dinner by my second day, but this was my battle. He had no connection with it. I was just a burden.

"All right." He leaped off the wall, seemingly renewed. Clapping his hands together, he turned those gleaming hazel eyes on me. "We need a place to stay. I don't know about you, but I'm dying for a bed. We just have to skirt our way around the night crowds and figure out where they keep their inns nowadays."

I nodded, and we started out of the alley. We didn't make it far. A dark form dropped from the rooftops, landing before us in a crouch. Before I could determine the barest details of the figure, it had Bay pinned and a cloth against his mouth. He slumped out of the person's smaller grasp and fell like a heap on the stones.

"Who are you?" I reached for my knife. In the instant

my attention drifted to Bay, hoping to catch a hint of movement, the being disappeared.

Hands knocked the wind out of me from behind, dredging into my gut. My knife slipped out of my grasp, and I gasped, inhaling a clinical, damp scent saturating a rag. Choking, my knees buckled, and I sagged against a soft body. Definitely, a woman.

In the final moments as my vision vanished and my mind shut off, all I could think about was the murder Bay had witnessed earlier. That woman's shrieking laughter echoed throughout my addled mind, and then there was nothing.

17TH NOVEMBER

I groaned awake, sore in my stomach. It took me several moments to remember what had happened, then I groaned again. Just another average day in Neverland, ending in horrors. Of course, it had been too calm; we needed the excitement of being kidnapped after doing nothing but slinking around all day.

Squinting through the darkness of the room, I tried to get my bearings. The space was empty, save for a flickering lantern several yards away. The floor was dirt, except for scattered rocks. Four pillars supported a structure above us, and Bay and I had been roughly tied to two of them. He was across the room at a diagonal, and his head still lolled to one side.

A jolt of panic shot through me, but in the dim light coming from the lantern, I could just see enough to know his chest moved.

"You're awake." Skye's voice made me jump, and I jerked my attention to the pixie. His large eyes were wide with worry. "How are you feeling? They gave you both an overdose." He looked at Bay, then back to me. "I've been trying to wake him for hours."

I wasn't doing great. I had the sense I needed to puke, but all I could do was gag. "How long have I been out?"

Skye wrung his hands. "Almost a day?"

"Shit," I blurted, trying to rub my face. Naturally, I couldn't because harsh ropes kept me firm against the wooden pillar. "Where's the woman?"

"No idea." His brows furrowed. "I snuck out when I couldn't hear movement anymore. She's been gone for a couple hours."

"Hopefully, not reporting to Hook," I mumbled. Skye's responding silence was all I needed to confirm that was a real concern. We had to get out of here. What if Hook did know?, Would he have enough honor to face me one-on-one. Even if I died trying, I'd die for Whisper's vengeance and provide enough distraction for Bay to get back to his own mission. "Can you untie me?"

Skye's brows nearly shot clean off his face. "Excuse me? Those ropes are thicker than my body? What do you think?"

"I think I've just been drugged," I snarled. "Give me a break."

Skye folded his arms. "If I had something sharp, I might be able to cut you loose, but they took Bay's knives, and I can't find a way out of here to look for anything else."

"Brilliant." I fought the tight coils wrapped around me to get a full breath, then I let it out slowly. "Okay.

Did they take my bag?" Hopefully not. There was nothing of importance in there.

"It's behind your pillar."

My eyes closed. "Thank the airwoman. There's a spyglass that I made in there. If you press on the glass part, it gets loose, and you can pop it out. It's sharp around the edges once it's free."

"Perfect." Skye brightened, zipping behind me. Shuffles ended in a crack that resonated in my soul.

"Did you break it?" I choked. I'd had that thing for years, dreaming of adventures I'd use it on. And I hadn't been alone when I'd made it. I'd been with Whisper. And though the "adventures" we'd used it on were childish, they were every bit as magical to me. If it was broken…

"No," he replied.

The coils of rope loosened, slipping away one by one, and I took a fuller breath, dragging myself back to the moment, the matter at hand. I clutched the feathers on my arm for strength and focused on Bay. "I can't carry him, so he needs to wake up, and—"

Wood thunked. I whirled. Skye vanished from sight.

The woman who had captured us dropped in through a trapdoor on the edge of the room, her gaze pinned on the ground before her. When she looked up, she caught my eye, and I stood frozen in place.

She hissed, "So, you're still here. And free now. Wonderful. I'm not in the mood for games." A cutlass, possibly Bay's, balanced in her hand, and she pointed the blade at me. "Drop your disguise, or I won't think twice about running you through."

At every turn, Neverland toyed with my mind,

twisting it until wounds broke open, raw and festering. I couldn't take it anymore. I was done with these games. I glared. I glared at her small, brown face, her fierce eyes, and disapproving lips. I glared at her limp curls of blond hair. I glared, willing Whisper to fall away into whatever horror was her true form.

"I mean it," she gritted. "Mom said to watch out for scum like you. I know what you are, so you can drop it."

"Likewise," I said, "I'm in a really shitty mood, so do your worst." I opened my arms to her. "I dare you."

She tightened her grip. "Explain him to me." Motioning with the blade, she flicked her gaze to Bay then back to me. "You, you, I get. But he's nothing to me. I met him for what, five minutes? I don't even remember his name at this point."

I dropped my arms. "What?"

Her nose scrunched, so flawlessly Whisper, it hurt. "You imprint upon my recent memories, and I've thought about you a damn lot, Lyly, but not him. In fact, you're a couple of idiots because if you'd really wanted to trick anyone, you'd have been my mom." Her anger heightened to a point I knew I was treading carefully. "I know Hook must employ you bastards, but I suppose only the morons are dumb enough to go into service."

Everything. Everything was perfect. Her tone. Her actions. Whisper stood before me, not her at all—I was certain of that—but whatever held her form had fished her mannerisms out of my head in the time I'd been asleep.

"Speaking of my mom," she growled, "where is she?"

"Dead." The word fell from my lips, leaving me

hollow. "She's dead. You're dead. Everything I've called family is gone."

"I know she's not dead," she spat, but her hand shook. "Hook needs her alive or the bait won't work on Peter because he won't remember who she is at all. I'm not an idiot! He could barely remember me at all." Her voice pitched, tears glassing her eyes in the lantern light. "Mom said it was because I was proof of something he hated, proof she had grown up, but still!"

I scoffed, but my throat closed. "He already forgot her. He forgot her in less than a day. Imagine that. Someone he'd known for a lifetime, gone in minutes."

"I said no games!"

"Kill me then!" I shouted. "You'll have to break character to do it! The girl you've stolen from my head has never hurt a single thing. I've watched her spend over an hour catching a moth in her house just to free it. She's vegetarian because it's too sad if animals have to die for her to eat. She once cried because her pet *caterpillar* died." Tears streamed down my cheeks, and I gasped. She'd named the stupid thing Fuzzy, and I'd sat with her while she cried.

Whisper hesitated, watching me with a wary gaze. Her voice was tiny when she spoke again. "That happened over eight years ago."

"Yeah. It did," I bit. "And yet dryocampa rubicunda is forever imprinted on my skull. Would it have killed you to call it a rosy maple moth? Because I don't think so."

Whisper covered her mouth with her free hand. "Lyly?" She swallowed, never releasing the sword. "Unless there's something other than a changeling that can take another's form, that's really you, isn't it?" She wet her lips. "Changelings can reach no further back than a year."

"Cute. I don't believe you, but the new tactic is endearing. You've had over a day to dig around in my unconscious brain, so who knows what you know."

Someone shifted behind me, then a groan filled the room. Mumbled curse words cut through our conversation. I had hoped that Skye would have Bay untied and at my side to figure this out before I found myself on the business end of a sword.

"Where's his pixie? Changelings don't have pixies." Whisper waved the sword around, then panicked. "Oh my airwoman, did I crush him in his coat?" She started for Bay, and my heart collided with my ribs.

Before I could think, I threw myself between them. "Don't touch him."

She blinked at me momentarily, then her mouth fell open. "No way." Her brows crashed together. "You got a boyfriend a week after you thought I died. I don't know whether to be proud or hurt."

I didn't know how to respond. There was no logical explanation on how she had managed to get here alive if she was really Whisper. None. But she had mentioned her mother, Tiger Lily, was here too. The last princess of Neverland.

There's always more than one way to get home.

"Skye," I snapped, my heart rate accelerating with a hope I knew would kill me if it ended up unfounded, "is that true? Only a year?"

A soft voice settled near me. "Yes, but if you've thought of it at all in this past year..."

"How do I tell, for sure." My words shook while I

stared at Whisper. *Please,* thrummed in my head, begging. Desperate. Another cruel trick. A better one than before. A much better one than before. Yet it was stuck inside my skull, giving me hope.

Whisper gasped, lifting the cutlass. I flinched, ready for all my hope to die with me, but she ran it across her finger, wincing when she shoved her hand at me. "See? Red."

There was a pause between us, then Skye muttered, "I mean. Yeah. That's a way. Changeling blood is black."

"Really?" I trembled. My voice wobbled. Tears filled my eyes and poured down my cheeks.

Before Skye could reply, I threw my arms around Whisper. The cutlass hit the dirt with a soft sound as she laughed and returned my hug. "It hasn't been that long, Lyly. But yikes. Okay. Yeah." She melted against me, her damp cheek against my shoulder. "I missed you too."

"You were dead," I choked on my sobs. "Dead."

"For a minute there, I thought I was. I have so much to tell you. Mom, well, she's kept a huge secret from us. I can't believe it."

"I know." I squeezed her, my laugh a garbled mess. "Did she tell you she was a princess?"

"No." Whisper scoffed. "She knows some magic, though! We're going to have a long talk once everything is back to normal. How in the world are you even here!"

"Is someone going to untie me…?" Bay mumbled. Everything but Whisper had fallen completely away, so much so I didn't remember he was even there until the moment he spoke. Without letting her go, I glanced at him, the goofiest smile on my face. He met it with a bleary cringe. "And tell me what's going on?"

"Whisper's *alive*. Somehow," I chimed. "But alive. And real. And right here."

Just as cheerily, Whisper added, "Also, Hook is alive and going to attack Skyla, using my mother to force Peter to tell him where the Fountain of Youth is."

The silence that followed was as still as death.

Continue the story in Throne of Feathers

A NOTE FROM THE AUTHOR

The Kingdom of Fairytales authors hope you enjoyed this new way of reading. We don't think that a series has ever been set with one chapter a day thought a whole year before and we hope we did it justice.

With this in mind, please leave a review, but when you do, remember that these books were always meant to be short breaks in your day and the blurb reflects that.

We would LOVE it if you can drop us a few words on Amazon

Review here

AFTER THE HAPPILY EVER AFTER...

There is more to these stories. You want to know what happens next right? Fast forward eighteen years...

Pick up book one now

PREQUEL

SLEEPING BEAUTY

1. Queen of Dragons
2. Heiress of Embers
3. Throne of Fury
4. Goddess of Flames

LITTLE MERMAID

5. Queen of Mermaids
6. Heiress of the Sea
7. Throne of Change
8. Goddess of Water

RED RIDING HOOD

9. King of Wolves
10. Heir of the Curse
11. Throne of Night
12. God of Shifters

RAPUNZEL

13. King of Devotion
14. Heir of Thorns
15. Throne of Enchantment
16. God of Loyalty

RUMPELSTILTSKIN

17. Queen of Unicorns
18. Heiress of Gold
19. Throne of Sacrifice
20. Goddess of Loss

BEAUTY AND THE BEAST

21. King of Beasts
22. Heir of Beauty
23. Throne of Betrayal
24. God of Illusion

ALADDIN

25. Queen of the Sun
26. Heiress of Shadows
27. Throne of the Phoenix
28. Goddess of Fire

CINDERELLA

29. Queen of Song
30. Heiress of Melody

31. Throne of Symphony
32. Goddess of Harmony

ALICE IN WONDERLAND

33. Queen of Clockwork
34. Heiress of Delusion
35. Throne of Cards
36. Goddess of Hearts

WIZARD OF OZ

37. King of Traitors
38. Heir of Fugitives
39. Throne of Emeralds
40. God of Storms

SNOW WHITE

41. Queen of Reflections
42. Heiress of Mirrors
43. Throne of Wands
44. Goddess of Magic

PETER PAN

45. Queen of Skies
46. Heiress of Stars
47. Throne of Feathers
48. Goddess of Air

URBIS

49. Kingdom of Royalty
50. Kingdom of Power
51. Kingdom of Fairytales
52. Kingdom of Ever After

JOIN US

Would you like to get Bay's adventure logs? Click the link below to pick your free gift up.

Kingdom of Fairytales FREE gift

Check the Kingdom of Fairytales website for competitions, news and info on all the books and authors

Kingdom of Fairytales Website

Or Join us on our Kingdom of Fairytales Facebook page for fun, games and author takeovers

Still want more? Completely immerse yourself in the Kingdom of Fairytales experience and pick up exclusive offers and gifts

Become a Patron

THE KINGDOM OF FAIRYTALES TEAM

These books would not be written without a great many people. Here is our team:

Many thanks to those who have made this possible.

Thank you to Rhi Parkes without whom, this series would never have come about.

Thanks to all the authors.

J.A. Armitage, Audrey Rich, B. Kristen Mcmichael, Emma Savant, Jennifer Ellision, Scarlett Kol, R. Castro, Margo Ryerkerk, Zara Quentin, Laura Greenwood and Anne Stryker

Also thank you to our amazing Beta team

Nadine Peterse-Vrijhof, Diane Major, Kalli Bunch and Stephanie Pittser.

Thanks to our Proof Reader

Tina Merritt

Thank you to our Patrons

Gigi Nickerson, Amanda Hurst & Coralee Butterfield

ABOUT J.A. ARMITAGE

J.A lives in a total fantasy world (because reality is boring right?) When she's not writing all the crazy fun in her head, she can be found eating cake, designing pretty pictures and hanging upside down from the tallest climbing frame in the local playground while her children look on in embarrassment. She's travelled the world working as everything from a banana picker in Australia to a Pantomime clown, has climbed to the top of Mount Kilimanjaro and the bottom of the Grand Canyon and once gave birth to a surrogate baby for a friend of hers.

She spends way too much time gossiping on facebook and if you want to be part of her Reading Army, where you'll get lots of freebies, exclusive sneak peeks and super secret sales, join up here

https://www.subscribepage.com/v7o8k4

Somehow she finds time to write.

ABOUT ANNE STRYKER

Anne Stryker was born and raised deep in the concrete garden of Jacksonville, Florida. As a Fantasy Romance author, Anne loves crafting fantastical worlds with swoony, humorous, or mysterious male leads and relatable main characters. Embracing the normal in the abnormal is her favorite pastime.

If you'd like to join her in her quest for Happily Ever Afters, you can find her on Instagram or you can join her Faerie Kaleidoscope by signing up to her mailing list:

Instagram: @AuthorAnneStryk

Faerie Kaleidoscope: http://eepurl.com/dGKJ6L

Printed in Great Britain
by Amazon

31657750R00071